Spiritual Pursuits
and other stories

Lien Chao

T0243946

MAWEN*Z*I
HOUSE

We acknowledge the support of the Canada Council for the Arts for our publishing program. We also acknowledge support from the Government of Ontario through the Ontario Arts Council, and the support of the Government of Canada through the Canada Book Fund.

Cover image: *Sunset on the Desert* 大漠落日 by Wang De Hui, 73cmx90cm, oil on canvas, 2005. Reproduced from *Wang De Hui* 王德惠. Ed. Wang Kun & Wang Shaoqiu. Hangzhou: China Academy of Fine Arts Publishing House, 2014.

Cover design by Sabrina Pignataro

Library and Archives Canada Cataloguing in Publication

Title: Spiritual pursuits and other stories / Lien Chao.
Names: Chao, Lien, 1950- author.
Identifiers: Canadiana (print) 20230230431 | Canadiana (ebook) 20230230458 | ISBN 9781774151006 (softcover) | ISBN 9781774151013 (EPUB) | ISBN 9781774151020 (PDF)
Subjects: LCGFT: Short stories.
Classification: LCC PS8555.H3955 S65 2023 | DDC C813/.54—dc23

Printed and bound in Canada by Coach House Printing

Mawenzi House Publishers Ltd.
39 Woburn Avenue (B)
Toronto, Ontario M5M 1K5
Canada
www.mawenzihouse.com

With gratitude to the Asian Heritage Month artists for creating and sharing with the public many high-quality, virtual programs during the COVID-19 shutdown of 2020-2022

CONTENTS

An Abiding Dream

Tiny white and violet flowers had appeared on the snow patches on the lawns. It was a sunny afternoon in March. A few sparrows were pecking for worms in the flower beds. Since the wind had lost its sharp edge, Ming and her seventy-five-year-old mother decided to go to Chinatown for grocery shopping. On the way to the subway station, Ming pointed at a black-capped chickadee sitting on top of the garden fence excitedly, "Mom, spring is definitely here!"

Mother and daughter planned to take the Spadina Street bus from the Bloor subway station, as these were days before streetcars were brought back to run the route. The bus was always crowded. Ming's mother sat on the seat next to the front door reserved for elders. When the bus curved around Spadina Crescent before reaching College Street, Ming had a sudden urge. It came to her from out of the blue, as if caused by the thrusting motion of the bus when it tried to make a stop. She felt she needed to drop by the small Chinese art gallery that was situated just south of Dundas Street.

It was a strange feeling. She could hardly remember the name of the gallery other than that it was something tawdry, having to do with beauty, as if it were a hair salon. She had visited the gallery several times in past years when she was in Chinatown with extra time to spare. This time there was no particular reason for visiting it except to take her mother there.

She dismissed the thought.

The bus pulled away from the College Street stop toward Chinatown and Dundas Street. "Mom, we'll get off at the next stop," Ming reminded her mother. From the bus windows, they could see the familiar signs of Chinese grocery stores where her mother liked to shop.

The bus braked again suddenly and she was lurched forward. And the thought returned.

"Mom, would you like to visit an art gallery first?" she asked.

Her mother looked surprised. "No, not today. Just want to buy some groceries. It's still chilly outside."

"Since you haven't been to Chinatown for several months, I thought maybe you would like to see some Chinese brush paintings for a change. After all, it's spring already," Ming said, trying to persuade her mother and herself at the same time.

Her mother looked confused, probably wondering why her daughter had suddenly changed their plan. While they were still talking, the bus stopped at Dundas Street. Most passengers got off and new ones noisily rushed on board, carrying multiple bags of groceries. For some strange reason, Ming's mother didn't get up from her seat before the bus pulled off again. Ming felt a gush of pleasure and she said to her mother, "Now, we can go to the art gallery before shopping for groceries!"

They got off at the next stop, close to the small art gallery. It was called Beauty and Modernity. "It does sound like a hair salon," she mumbled with a chuckle. The gallery had a side entrance. When Ming pulled the door open, she couldn't see the interior, but she could hear a man speaking loudly with a northern Chinese accent.

"I want to talk to him," Ming said to her mother.

"Who?"

"The man who is talking loudly."

"You know him?" asked her mother curiously.

"No, not yet," answered Ming honestly. She didn't know how to tell her mother about her impulse. Ming's mother gave her daughter a not-so-funny look as if to question her sanity.

Stepping into the one-room gallery, they saw two men in their sixties having a conversation in the middle of the room, one with long white hair tied up into a ponytail behind his head and the other with a short stubby haircut. The white-haired man continued his speech.

"Fifty years after oil painting was initially introduced to China from the West, it has been accepted and adopted by Chinese artists and audiences. It is taught in all the fine-art departments in Chinese universities and displayed in art galleries across the country. Many Chinese audiences like oil painting more than Chinese brush painting. Why can't Chinese brush painting be accepted in the West?"

Ming stared at the white-haired man, provoked by his question. Why? She didn't know. The other man shrugged his shoulders. "Perhaps Chinese brush painting is too traditional for contemporary audiences to relate to."

"Maybe, but art is visual. If we educate the audience, especially the younger generation and help them gain some basic knowledge about Chinese art mediums, gradually they would be able to appreciate them." The two men walked toward the door still discussing.

Ming's mother was looking at the paintings on the wall. Standing behind her mother, Ming felt anxious. "I think this is a print from a limited edition," said Ming to her mother, her voice a little loud.

Both men immediately turned around curiously to watch the two visitors.

"You are right, young lady, they are prints," said the white-haired man. "Are you artists, yourselves?"

"Yes, we are," Ming responded, "My mother does Chinese brush painting, specializing in birds and flowers, I am a portrait artist."

"We love to talk to fellow artists," the guys looked at each other, then instead of leaving the gallery, as they had intended, they stepped back and placed four chairs in front of the window.

"Please sit down," one of them said.

So they did. Ming faced the white-haired man, who introduced himself as Big Brush, and her mother faced the stubby-haired guy, Old Ox.

The rest of the afternoon the four of them sat there and talked passionately. They talked about where they came from, what they had done in the past, why they had come to Canada, and what they had dreamt to do in Canada.

Dusk fell outside the window. Chinatown turned on its colourful neon lights. Inside the gallery, the fluorescent lighting became much brighter. "It's too late to go grocery shopping!" Ming's mother sighed. Facing the window, Ming saw another Spadina bus pulling away from the bus stop.

In the following weeks, Big Brush introduced Ming to other artists in Chinatown. They met regularly on Tuesday afternoons for tea at the Golden Gate Bakery on Dundas Street. Most of them spoke Cantonese. Ming switched between Mandarin and English as she tried to keep up with them. She met Old Mo, a calligrapher, seal-carver, and amateur photographer. Mo generously promised to make Ming a personal seal in the near future. Ming also had a good talk with Old Horse, a sophisticated Chinese brush painter from Taiwan, a widow whose husband had been a Kuomintang general. In her late seventies, Old Horse had been teaching Chinese brush painting to a dozen private Caucasian students, who had been with her for more than two decades. For the weekly casual gathering, local artists brought their recent artwork to show to each other, asking for comments; and they also looked for potential buyers from those who dropped by the tea lounge behind the bakery on Tuesday afternoons.

A teapot of green tea plus a piece of pastry would last a couple of hours, the teapot getting refilled several times. The owner of the bakery knew most of the artists and greeted them in person as they came in. Big Brush seemed to know all the artists.

"Do you speak Cantonese?" Ming asked.

"No, not really, maybe a couple of words," smiled Big Brush.

"Then how do you communicate with your friends?"

"Through brush strokes and calligraphic lines," Big Brush continued to smile as if it wasn't a problem, "painting is visual."

On Canada Day, Chinatown organized a community celebration dinner banquet in a restaurant called International City Restaurant on Dundas Street. Big Brush, Old Ox, Old Horse, Old Rock, and other artists put together an exhibition of Chinese brush painting on the wall. Several hundred people attended that evening. Ming was invited as a guest of the artists. There were thirty-five tables altogether each with ten people. The small stage was decorated with a Canadian flag and an Ontario provincial flag; a red banner hanging across the stage written in huge Chinese calligraphy style declared, "Chinatown Celebrating Canada Day."

It was Ming's first time to attend a dinner event in Chinatown. To her surprise, eminent politicians were present as well. It dawned on Ming that downtown Chinatown played a much more important role in Toronto than she had been aware of. In addition to providing convenient grocery stores for the locals, a number of

Chinese restaurants served excellent traditional Chinese cuisine to attract tourists and Torontonians year round. Chinatown has also been an important gathering place for politicians to reach out to the Chinese community, and vice versa.

It was a hot July evening. Heat seemed to have doubled in intensity when the loudspeakers were turned on high to sing "O Canada." Clearing her throat, Ming quickly caught up with the crowd for "True patriot love in all thy sons command" when she heard people standing beside her singing different lyrics. She stopped instinctively to listen to Mr Ng, a community leader who was singing in front of the microphone on the stage. He was actually singing the national anthem in Cantonese! People standing solemnly beside each table were also following the lyrics in Chinese from a printout in their hands.

A bilingual emcee, speaking perfect English and Cantonese, introduced the Minister of Travel and Tourism, who paid tribute to the Chinese community for making great contributions to Canada. He ended his short speech with a few words in Cantonese. A thunderous applause burst out from the floor. Ming clapped her hands as well, wondering whether the Minister had just said Gong-Hei-Fa-Cai, the only Cantonese phrase she knew for the Chinese New Year.

Mr Ng came back to the stage to shake hands with the minister; he also brought to the stage a framed Chinese brush painting. The emcee came to the microphone and called out Mr Brush's name, first in Cantonese and then in English. Big Brush stood up from his seat and went up to the stage radiating under the spot lights. Mr Ng introduced him to the Minister who shook his hand warmly. Then Mr Ng brought forward the painting. Big Brush and the Minister both held up the painting to show to the audience. Cameras flashed.

When Big Brush came back to their table looking proud and dignified, the whole table gave him a standing ovation.

"Congratulations, Mr Brush! We are proud of you! Now your painting has become part of the provincial government's collection, the Minister will certainly help you get into the mainstream," announced Old Ox. "The minister's secretary had asked for a painting by the best artist in Chinatown. There you are."

"Thank you, thank you, that's too much honour," Big Brush waved his right hand from left to right. He blushed and his eyes were shining wetly.

After more speeches, a grand ten-course Chinese banquet started to roll out from the kitchen to the hall. The first entrée was a large platter of Chinese BBQ cold cuts, pork ribs, beef slices, chicken and duck pieces as well as transparent jellied fish strips sprinkled with roasted sesame seeds. The cold platter was followed by hot dishes of steamed fish, stir-fried garlic shrimp, twin lobsters in ginger and onion, a crispy smoked chicken, and so on. Uniformed servers rushed up and down the aisles and among the tables in such a hurry that Ming wondered how they remembered which table had been served any particular dish.

From time to time, she stood up to take a peek at the head table, where the politicians were sitting. They were eating and chatting among themselves as if attending a private dinner. After the ten courses had been served, they bid each other goodbye and departed.

When all the guests had left, Ming stayed behind to help the artists take down the paintings and calligraphies on display. Mr Ng, who had introduced Big Brush to the minister, walked down from the stage, looking quite satisfied.

"Congratulations, Mr Brush, your painting went to the provincial government's office on behalf of the community. Here is the certificate signed by the Minister of Travel and Tourism." He handed Big Brush a green folder. Big Brush opened the folder and held it up proudly for Ming and the others to see. It was an official Queen's Park certificate signed by the MPP for the Canada Day celebration.

"Did the minister buy the painting?" asked Ming curiously, "They had asked for a Chinese brush painting by the best painter in Chinatown."

Mr Ng and Big Brush turned pale and stared at Ming for a long minute. "What did you say?" Mr Ng asked. The broad smile had disappeared from his face.

Ming could see that she had offended the two men by having said something insulting. What she really wanted to know was whether Chinatown artists could make a living as artists, and whether there was a market for their paintings.

A few organizers were lowering the banner from above the stage and packing up the sound system. The paintings were taken down one by one from the wall and rolled into tubes, revealing a bare and dirty wall. A vacuum cleaner started to roar back and forth on the carpet, and the lights were dimmed.

It turned out that most of the artists in Chinatown couldn't make a living with their art. Some artists took private students, some were supported by their grown-up children, others were spending whatever was left of the money they had brought to Canada. Those without personal or family resources lived on government welfare. The best scenario would be when they reached sixty-five years and could apply for the Guaranteed Income Supplement and Old Age Security pension.

"Guys, do you think we artists should be able to support ourselves with our work?" Ming posed the question one day at the Golden Gate Bakery for Tuesday afternoon tea.

"A good question," Old Ox responded with a wry smile. "Some of us did that in China for many years, right, Big Brush?"

The latter nodded. "But in Canada we face many barriers. First of all, we don't speak very much English . . . and then, we work with Chinese brush painting."

"But you said art is visual. As long as the audience can see the paintings, they should be able to appreciate it." Ming reminded Big Brush of what he often said.

"It takes several generations of artists to bring up a generation of appreciative audiences and potential art collectors. We need to start sharing our art form through the education system in Canada," Big Brush said.

Another time, Ming asked a totally different question. "Can you guys sketch?"

"Sketching? I taught sketching for years in China," answered Big Brush. He said sketching was one of the most important courses that all fine art students had to take in the first year. Since artists were often teachers and professors in China, they didn't need to worry about making a living in those days. In Canada, people thought being an artist meant a choice of lifestyle for an escapist, who didn't want to hold a regular job.

"If you can sketch, I know how you can make a living," Ming said.

Two weeks later, in front of Toronto's Eaton Centre at the corner of Yonge and Dundas Streets, the busiest street corner of this cosmopolitan city, a Chinese man and woman were standing on the sidewalk, with sketching boards in their hands. There were many other solicitors at the corner, including food vendors and musicians, but these two were the only artists.

"Portrait! Do you want a portrait?"

"Do you want a portrait?"

"Twenty dollars for a portrait, only twenty!"

"If you don't like it, you don't have to buy it."

Not too far from where the two Chinese artists were standing, parked closer to the curb was a hot dog cart. A young couple had just stopped there and ordered the street food. A swirl of white smoke was ascending the rotating silver aluminum chimney above the roof of the hot dog stand.

Ming went up to the young woman. "Hello, would you like a portrait?" She held up a sample portrait of Marilyn Monroe in colour pastel.

"Did you do that?" the young woman asked, her eyes wide open, shining with delight and surprise.

"Yes, I did," answered Ming proudly.

"How long did it take you to do such a nice portrait?"

"A good hour."

Their hot dogs were ready. The couple started squeezing ketchup and mustard bottles, putting on slices of pickles, onions, and hot pepper rings.

Ming waited patiently for a few minutes. When the couple took their first bites, she pointed at the four white deck chairs she and Big Brush had set down for their customers. "You are welcome to take a seat, please sit down."

"Could we?"

"Of course." She made a gesture of invitation.

The couple sat down on the deck chairs and looked at the sample portraits displayed on the sidewalk.

Ming quietly picked up her sketch board and did an outline of the young woman's face with a piece of charcoal. When she focused on the woman's face, she could see her long eyelashes curling upward, her slightly long nose, her white teeth, and her sandy brown hair hanging down to her shoulders in soft wavy curls.

"Michael Jordan, my favourite basketball star!" the young man exclaimed, picking up a portrait in colour pastel from the sidewalk.

"He is also a Jordan fan," Ming pointed at Big Brush. "He did the portrait."

When the couple finished their hot dogs, Ming was ready to put her sketch of the young woman behind a matte board frame with a semitransparent covering sheet. "Take a look at your portrait," she handed her work politely to the young woman.

"Oh, my God," screamed the young woman. "Did you draw this just now? I can't believe it! Look at this, Sweetie," she handed the portrait to the young man.

"Wow, it's you! This is definitely you! The eyes have got your spirit, and I like the long curls of your hair covering up part of the face," commented the young man with admiration.

"This is so incredible! You did my portrait while I was eating the hot dog. But it was such a short time. Can I buy it from you?"

"If you like it, it's twenty dollars."

"Certainly," answered the young woman.

The couple wanted the woman's portrait and also Michael Jordan's. Ming knew that Big Brush probably wouldn't want to sell his favourite Jordan portrait, but it was too late. The young man handed her two twenty-dollar bills.

"Thank you very much," said Ming. She couldn't believe that she had just made a sale of their artwork.

Big Brush rubbed his hands excitedly, "I can't believe this, Ming, you did it!"

"Yes, we did it. We made twenty dollars each in half an hour, not bad, eh? That's forty dollars an hour, very high pay in the labour market today." Ming laughed, passing a twenty-dollar bill to her fellow artist.

"No, no, you keep the money," Big Brush waved away her offer. "After all, you did all the talking." He wasn't too sure how this had happened, two strangers had stopped for hot dogs and also paid for his work.

"You must take the money," Ming said firmly. "Because you need to get used to having people pay you for your work." She squeezed the twenty-dollar bill into his jacket pocket.

Blushing, the old artist felt embarrassed to let a young woman take care of him. Back in China, he could probably be the professor teaching her how to improve her drawing, but as a newcomer in Canada, this young woman seemed to know her way around and now she wanted to introduce him to a new career as a street artist. To make a living was important to all newcomers in Canada, and that included artists. He decided to work with her for now until he could find a way to have his paintings displayed on brightly lit art gallery walls instead of selling sketches to pedestrians beside a hot dog stand. But still, he couldn't believe that he had started a brand-new business on the main street of Toronto.

"How did you know that portraits would sell on the street?" Big Brush asked Ming curiously.

"Many artists have done it in New York City, so have I."

In the early 1980s, a few years after China's leader Chairman Mao passed away, his successors decided to open the nation's door a little wider to the West. Some friendly foreigners were hired to teach English at selected Chinese universities, and at the same time the country sent out its first batch of visiting scholars and overseas students.

Ming was a young artist among the second group. She carried thirty-five US dollars of her own money, the amount of foreign currency that the Chinese government allowed a citizen to take out of the country. Ming thought she was never so well equipped financially because the amount constituted her three months' salary as a university lecturer. When she showed her family and friends the American dollars, the crispy bills were passed around from hand to hand, to be scrutinized by curious eyes and admired by envious hearts.

"What can you buy with thirty-five American dollars?" asked her friends. "A TV, a refrigerator, maybe a bicycle?"

"I have no idea."

It took Ming less than twenty-four hours in New York City to find out the value of thirty-five American dollars. She learned that renting a basement room in Chinatown cost three hundred dollars a month; the tuition for the art school she had signed up for was another three hundred a month. Adding food and transportation, her minimum monthly expenses could easily exceed one thousand dollars, an astronomical sum in the early 1980s for a Chinese student without financial resources.

In order to survive, she immediately took a part-time job at a garment factory in the basement of a warehouse. She was assigned to work on a sewing machine. She could make twenty-four dollars a day working for eight hours. At the end of her first week, when she received her first week's pay in cash, she was warmly congratulated by fellow illegal workers for the fact that she had survived and made a living on her own in America! But as a full-time worker, she could not attend art school. For the next three months, she sewed thousands of buttons, paid her rent, and saved a few hundred dollars. She did other low-paying jobs in the illegal labour market such as waitressing in a Chinese restaurant or at an Asian supermarket as a cashier. But if all her efforts were just to survive in New York at the expense of her artistic career, why should she have come to America?

On a Saturday evening Ming decided to go to Greenwich Village, about which she had heard, to investigate America's own starving artists. Following a map in her hands, she went to Washington Square. She was immediately attracted to a rambunctious scene: street musicians were playing Latin American music and had attracted a large crowd. Ming stood behind the crowd to watch. From time to time, someone in the audience stepped inside the circle to drop a quarter or two into a small white bucket on the ground. Occasionally, a few people dropped a bill. Ming couldn't tell how much the bills were since American paper money looked the same to her.

After a good hour, the musicians took a break and people started to disperse. Ming moved on to the next scene. Two jugglers were catching falling balls and bottles; they sure knew how to tease the audience. With gestures to indicate they might just miss the falling objects, they made the onlookers scream. One of the jugglers came forward to collect from the crowd. Most of the people dropped something into the baseball cap in his hand. Ming took a peep inside when it came to her and was surprised to see that some fifty to sixty dollars had already been collected.

Ming passed a candle-lit restaurant where people were holding wine glasses, pop cans, or coffee cups while listening to a man with messy long hair reading from some loose manuscript sheets. The guy looked like a poet. Ming vaguely remembered the name of Bob Dylan. Was Dylan a famous poet or songwriter who once lived in Greenwich Village? She tiptoed into the restaurant and leaned against the back wall. She wanted to catch a few words, a poetic line, so she could share the inspiration of being an artist in New York. But she couldn't figure out a single line from where she was standing.

Walking further west towards the famous gay havens and bars, Ming suddenly saw what she was actually looking for—visual artists. A dozen of them, black and white, young and middle-aged men, had spread out their work on the sidewalk. Two were standing talking to onlookers; a few were sitting in plastic deck chairs with sketch boards on their laps, drawing portraits of customers sitting across from them. Sample portraits were displayed on the sidewalk facing up.

Comparing the scene to the live model-sketching classes at her university in China, Ming thought the street lighting was perhaps too dim for the artists to see the details of their models, but it didn't seem to matter at all, they only needed to look up at the models for a moment or two.

Suddenly Ming felt an unusual warmth of excitement growing inside her body. For the first time since she had landed in America, she sensed intuitively that she had finally arrived at the door of her future—not the art school that she had originally signed up for, but the streets of New York where she would practice her art by sketching and drawing ordinary Americans.

Big Brush held his breath while listening to Ming's reminiscences. Having been a professor of fine arts for thirty years in China, he had no idea about how different it could be for artists to survive on the streets in New York or Toronto. Now this young artist, twenty years his junior at least, was courageous enough to have found a way to make a decent living from her art. He was truly moved, but would he forsake his lifetime practice of Chinese brush painting in order to survive? He didn't think his life would be the same or even worth living any more if he decided to become a street artist for the rest of his life.

"Did you join the portrait artists in Greenwich Village?" asked Big Brush.

"Yes, I did," answered Ming excitedly.

Big Brush looked at the young woman suspiciously; to him Ming was too naïve to understand life. "Did the local American artists accept you? Wouldn't they regard you as a competitor, if not a threat?"

"In fact, they welcomed me to join them. Old Jackson, a Black artist, even gave me his extra portfolio carrier. Kevin and David, two young artists, helped me find foldable deck chairs from a furniture dump behind the townhouses in the Village. They were willing to share their business with me. Isn't that incredible?"

Big Brush didn't respond. He couldn't believe that Americans would not be as jealous as some Chinese he knew would be in a similar situation. "So, could you make a living in New York as a street artist?"

Ming started to make sixty to a hundred dollars a day as a portrait artist in Greenwich Village. She told Big Brush she never needed to go back to her old jobs.

Soon word spread among newcomer artists in New York that a Chinese artist had found a better way to make a living. She had earned more money than working extra shifts washing dishes in the restaurants or sewing buttons in garment factories. Many Chinese artists came to Greenwich Village, looking for Ming and a better life. Some of them even arrived with one hand pulling a luggage cart loaded with two foldable chairs, the other hand carrying a portfolio case.

Two months after Ming had become a portrait artist in the Village, suddenly there were too many of them. It became too competitive to make a living, and so a group of them, including Ming and her boyfriend David Goodwin, whom she had met in the business, decided to move to another location.

This time they decided to set up their business in Times Square—the heart of New York City, where millions of tourists from all over the world come to visit every year and thousands of Americans gather ritually on New Year's Eve. Ming had watched the New Year's celebration on TV before. But never had she dared to imagine setting up her own art business on one of the most famous public squares in the world.

On a September evening, Ming and David marched to Times Square, each pulling a two-wheeled luggage dolly loaded with two folded chairs and small easels. As they stepped onto the Square, Ming screamed at the top of her lungs for the historic turning point of their portrait business. She remembered an old Chinese saying, which was so relevant to what they were doing: "Hey, David, guess what the Chinese say about the first person who dared to eat crabs in human history?"

David stopped in his tracks. "They said the guy was crabby."

Ming laughed loudly, shaking her head, "No, no! They said the first person who dared to eat crabs had guts!"

"I see—, that's so true!" Scratching his head, David said loudly, "We sure have guts!"

South of Times Square on 42nd Street was the famous red-light district, and north of the Square on 45th Street were the famous theatres. Sex and art enticed businesses and mixed crowds, and well-dressed theatregoers brushed shoulders with hookers and flower girls on the same sidewalks. Police patrols frequented the area, arriving from time to time to chase away small vendors, prostitutes, vagabonds, drinkers, addicts, and drug dealers.

It was a beautiful fall evening. A cool breeze blew gently across the Square without stirring up any dust under the streetlights. After a police patrol had left the block, the portrait artists quickly set up their stands. Within an hour, every one of them had found a client to work with.

"The cops are back!" someone shouted. Within minutes, Ming saw a long shadow cast on the sidewalk at her back. Ming could only continue to sketch. Too scared to turn around, she tried her best to stay calm, hoping that her client would remain as calm and let her finish the portrait. For the next fifteen minutes, she worked with the policeman's long shadow on the sidewalk beside her. It was unreasonable to expect that police officer was seriously interested in her sketching. Time had frozen in Times Square until she had finally finished the portrait. She didn't know what to say or do next. Perhaps the cop would confiscate her work and even her material.

"That's it," she said nervously, putting down her charcoal stick.

"You have forgotten to draw a mustache," the policeman remarked behind her.

"Ha, ha, ha . . . " the Black woman who was her client burst out laughing, as did the other onlookers.

Ming was too stunned to understand what the policeman had said. She could only feel the cool evening breeze on her wet T-shirt that was soaked through with her sweat.

It turned out that the police in Times Square treated the portrait artists differently from other street vendors. With a friendly attitude, they chose to keep one eye open and one eye closed to let the portrait artists make a living in the belly of Times Square.

News spread like a spring breeze. Soon more Chinese artists left Greenwich Village and rushed to Times Square. Here, surrounded by skyscrapers and blinking neon lights, they had the world's largest live portrait-sketching classroom in the history of Western art. Faces of all human races showed up here, all skin tones and colours were available. Some models were beautiful; others were rough-looking. The artists usually worked from early afternoon to midnight. Occasionally when business was good, Ming and David would work throughout the night until dawn. When they finally stood up to receive the first ray of sunshine in Times Square, they embraced each other, "We did it. We did it!"

Making a living was no longer a problem. Soon Ming thought she would like to publish a collection of her work. Her working title was "Portraits of American People." She started to look for various models from the variety of people passing through the Square. Most of the time the people she selected acquiesced to her request to sketch them.

Two weeks after Big Brush and Ming started their portrait-sketching on the sidewalk outside Toronto's Eaton Centre, other artists came to join them. Their number grew rapidly at this intersection until one morning they counted thirty-five of them. They spread out on a long line along the sidewalk on Yonge Street, each with two foldable chairs and wooden easels. Sample portraits placed high on the easels or low on the sidewalk presented an impressive outdoor art show. Ming noted that this location was even better than Times Square for portrait business because the sidewalk was not only three times wider, but also in the shade throughout the afternoon.

The majority of the portrait artists came from mainland China, but there were others from Romania, Bulgaria, South America, and the Middle East. All of them were new immigrants to Canada. Like Ming and Big Brush, they had not been able to make a living as artists, and so they were grateful to these two Chinese artists for their initiative.

Big Brush said generously, "We are all entitled to make a living with our skills. The sidewalk belongs to the city, therefore we can all share it."

One rainy day, when the portrait artists had gathered inside a nearby Chinese noodle house, Big Brush asked, "Wasn't Leonardo da Vinci a portrait artist among his many other talents?"

"Of course, he was," someone responded, mentioning da Vinci's famous self-portrait in red chalk.

"And wasn't his painting, the *Mona Lisa*, one of the most expensive paintings in the world?" Big Brush continued, "Do you know the painting was actually a portrait of an unidentified woman?"

"Wow, Professor Brush, it is a portrait indeed!"

"Who were the models for Vincent van Gogh?"

"He painted the portraits of his postman and his neighbours." Young artists loved to answer Big Brush's questions as if they were his students.

With satisfaction and true delight on his face, Big Brush said emotionally, "So don't belittle yourselves. You are making a decent living with your skills like other professionals."

One afternoon in early August, the artists were working as usual on the sidewalk outside Eaton Centre. Two police officers walked down the block. They asked the two artists working closest to the intersection for their personal IDs, and then gave them each a yellow ticket with a hundred-dollar fine for violating the city's bylaw. The artists refused to take the tickets, so the officers left the tickets on their chairs. Other artists working further south on the sidewalk could see trouble coming. A few without customers quickly grabbed their gear and ran inside the Centre to hide. The rest stood there, scratching their heads, wondering what was suddenly happening.

"Why are they ticketing us? What's going on?" they asked each other anxiously.

The next day, the officers returned and gave tickets to two other artists. The group started to panic. Fear seized them. What had they done wrong? What law had they violated? They hadn't blocked any traffic, so why had they been ticketed? They couldn't concentrate on their work when they had to constantly look out for cops.

"It's not worth it. Hundred dollars could be two days' work for me," Mr Said commented, "I am quitting."

"What the hell is going on, Brush?" asked Mr Man, nicknamed Super Man, having had several physical fights with other artists for a spot closer to the intersection. Later Big Brush had to adopt a fair queuing system by switching the first two artists at the head of the line to the end of the queue the next day in order to give every artist an opportunity to work in the good spots. Now that the cops were more likely to ticket the artists working closer to the intersection, Super Man didn't want the spot any more, not even when it was his turn to work at the head of the line. He quietly asked Ming whether she would be so kind as to take his spot. Ming looked at Big Brush for advice; Big Brush laughed and said to Super Man, "At the end of the day, you may regret not making enough money."

"No, I won't, I promise you," answered Super Man firmly and without any hesitation or embarrassment. Big Brush moved his gear up the line. "Salute!" Super Man saluted Ming and Big Brush. Whoever dared to work closer to the intersection won the highest esteem from fellow artists. Setting up their stands near the intersection, Big Brush and Ming went to City Hall to find out the reason behind the ticketing.

Shortly after their departure, a policeman came down the street, swinging his body from side to side. When he saw no artists working at the first two spots, but only chairs and tools, he went down the line to pick his victim. He passed all the male artists working in the long line as if he didn't see them and went straight up to Pan Ling, a female artist who had been in Canada for only two weeks. Pan Ling stood up timidly from her chair to show respect.

"Your license?" The cop stretched out his hand.

Pan Ling didn't understand the word "license." She stretched out her two empty hands to show the officer that she had nothing to show him.

"I repeat. Your license," barked the policeman.

Pan Ling didn't know what to do. She turned around asking fellow artists for help and at the same time, she gave the police officer a polite, apologetic smile and two empty hands.

"Are you smiling?" he demanded. "Are you challenging me?" he said to Pan Ling impatiently, indicating that she should come with him.

Pan Ling followed the policeman inside Eaton Centre, then down and through a long underground tunnel, and eventually they came out above the ground near a low-rise cement building that looked like a square warehouse. Above the entrance of the building she saw the street number 250 and three large Chinese characters in white paint 警察局 [*jing cha ju*], meaning The Police Bureau.

She panicked. What had she done? Was she under arrest? Would they deport her back to China? The thought was a nightmare. She had just escaped from China a month before the pro-democracy movement was suppressed by military force at Tiananmen Square. In order to come to Canada to be reunited with her husband, she had made a long journey via Thailand. She understood that her rights were protected in Canada. How could a policeman just arrest her? And how could she defend herself without knowing much English?

Once inside the Police Bureau, the officer handed Pan Ling to a female officer for body search. Pan Ling had only an eraser, a piece of charcoal, and a subway token in her pockets. Then the white officer brought in a young Chinese officer who started speaking Cantonese to her. Pan Ling shook her head, didn't the police force know Chinese don't always speak the same dialect? The Chinese officer went back to using body language; he shrugged his shoulders and stretched out his empty hands to indicate his helplessness. Pan Ling did the same. The Chinese officer then dialed a number on the office telephone before passing the receiver to her.

From the other end of the line came a soft female voice speaking Mandarin. Pan Ling was overjoyed, she felt a surge of emotion rushing through her entire body. She wanted to hold on to that voice. She wanted to tell the voice in her mother tongue how she had escaped China as a sympathizer of the students' pro-democracy movement. She also wanted to share with the voice how difficult it had been for a newcomer, an artist, to find a job in Canada, and how she had found out about the portrait artists on Yonge Street and decided to join them. She had so much to tell the mother-tongue voice, her shaky hands gripping tightly onto the receiver as if it were a real person. But before she could say a single word in her native language, tears came down from her eyes and sorrow blocked her throat, and she burst out sobbing.

"Please don't cry," the soft voice consoled her, "tell me what happened today."

Pan Ling poured out her story. Her voice was charged with a woman artist's extra frustration and indignation. She had never talked so vigorously before, but she did it today to defend her rights and her innocence. She could tell that the woman at the other end was attentive, until she was told to pass the receiver to the police officer.

When Pan Ling returned to the Yonge/Dundas intersection, her fellow artists gave her a standing ovation on the sidewalk. After she told them what had happened in the Police Bureau, Super Man gave her a military salute. Big Brush and Ming had just returned from City Hall. Ming hugged Pan Ling tightly before telling the group about the latest troubles they had with the police tickets and Pan Ling's arrest. It turned out that Eaton Centre had filed a complaint against the portrait artists for trespassing, especially on rainy days, dirtying their lobby and disrupting their business.

"We shouldn't have used their lobby as a shelter from the rain," said Big Brush regretfully.

"But where can we go when it rains?" Mr Said asked.

"And we did make a mess in their lobby," continued Big Brush.

"We have equipment, we couldn't help it," Mr Said added angrily. "Shouldn't they show some understanding?"

"The fact is we did make a mess in their lobby," Ming reminded the artists. "They have their rights to complain to the city."

"And for this small matter, the damned Eaton wants to take away our rice bowl," Super Man cried out. "I feel like smashing its damned glass windows to teach the stinky rich Eaton a lesson," he added.

"Please control yourself!" Big Brush raised his voice. "Don't forget this is Canada, not your Cultural Revolution in China. It is illegal to trespass on private property. Although we have our right to make a living, we can't violate other people's rights. So, what should we do as a group of law-abiding residents of the city?" Big Brush asked the question seriously.

In the end, the portrait artists decided to write a petition to protest against Eaton Centre's unreasonable demand to remove them from working at the intersection. Ming's English appeared to be better than others', so she undertook the task, spending half a day drafting the petition.

Ming read the petition to the group. Thirty-five artists raised their voices and waved their arms to sign their names. The group also decided to take a day off to hold a public protest in order to collect signatures from tourists and Toronto residents passing this busy downtown intersection.

It was a beautiful Saturday in early August. The artists brought their best work to make Yonge Street at Dundas a much brighter spot for tourists and local residents. The portraits on display were created in almost all art mediums, pencil, charcoal, colour pastels, acrylic, and oil paint; there was print-making, paper-cutting, and Chinese brush painting on *Xuan* paper. They displayed portraits of recognizable multiracial celebrities as well as ordinary people. Big Brush told fellow artists that they were responsible for passing their best artwork to the next two generations in order to keep the portrait art form alive at the grass roots for the next four hundred years.

Tourists and locals crowded in front of the portrait exhibition, chatting with the artists. People lined up to sign a petition on behalf of the artists and many offered suggestions as to how to solve the dispute.

Later that year, City Hall held several public hearings and consultations. The portrait artists were welcomed to sit in as a group. At each session Ming presented more signatures from supporters of their petition. The majority of the city councillors supported the artists, and so in the end a motion of compromise was passed stating that the portrait market could stay at this city block, but the artists would need licenses to work, just like other vendors. The license would be valid for one year and only twenty-six licenses would be issued each year for that spot so that the intersection would not become overcrowded. While working on the sidewalk at this intersection, the artists would be strictly forbidden to use Eaton Centre as a shelter or temporary storage.

"We are going to stay!" The portrait artists waved their arms and shouted. "We won!"

"Wait a minute," Super Man said. "We didn't really win, the rich buggers won in the end. Didn't you guys hear the licensing system? What that means is that nine of us lose our rice bowl and starve! Damn it, you guys didn't see what was coming?"

"This is Canadian politics, there is no true right or wrong. The winner and the loser both win something and lose something," Said commented.

Prior to the beginning of the new system, the portrait artists unanimously agreed to draw lots for the twenty-six licensed spots. Thirty-five artists went to a nearby Chinese restaurant for their last all-member meeting. Over a cup of jasmine tea and crispy spring rolls, they each drew from a Blue Jays cap held in Ming's hands.

"Who hasn't drawn from the cap?" Super Man asked anxiously before taking his. There were still two folded papers inside the cap.

Ming glanced at Big Brush, who looked back at her with a nod.

"I decided to give up my chance," Big Brush announced quietly.

"So did I," Ming followed.

After the first round of draws, twenty-four artists got the licenses. What this meant was that if Ming and Big Brush had taken their draws, they would have gotten the remaining two licenses.

"Damn it," Super Man's fist came down on the table, announcing that he got a blank note.

"There is a second chance for those who got a blank," Ming said cheerfully. After calculating the number of possible draws, she folded up seven more blank papers in the same way as she had prepared for the first round of draws and put them back inside the cap with the two remaining draws. She shook them up.

"Good luck, everyone," she said and gestured to the nine artists who had drawn a blank in the first round to come forward. Three of them went up for their second pick.

"I got one!" Said exclaimed, holding his note up. "I will get a license! My family will be fed, thank you, Big Brush and Ming for your generosity!"

Super Man's eyes were closed. He was murmuring something that nobody understood. He then walked towards Ming, eyes still closed, his hands stretched in front of him as if he were blind. Ming put the cap in front of him; his right hand touched the brim of the cap and then dipped inside. His eyes remained closed as his hand picked up a note.

Super Man opened his eyes a bit and held up the paper before him. With both hands, slowly and solemnly, he unfolded the note one side at a time. The other artists remained quietly seated, holding their breath, waiting for the result. Ming was glad she had followed Big Brush's decision to give up her opportunity to a family man or woman. Since she was single, it would be easier for her to get by. And now watching Super Man behave in such an abnormal way, instead of his usual aggressiveness, Ming suddenly had a surge of affection for the guy. There was only one license left, and she wished him good luck.

"All mercy, Avalokitesvara," Super Man knelt down in front of the crowd and kissed the note in his hands. He didn't really give a glance at the note before passing it to Ming.

Ming took the note from him and looked at it. "Hey, Man, congratulations! You have drawn the last license!" She said excitedly.

"I did? Did I? Really?" Super Man opened his eyes wide, Ming could see tears running down from his sunken eyes. "Thank you, Brush, my Buddha, and Ming, you are a beautiful Bodhisattva. My family thanks you for your kindness!" He grabbed Big Brush's hands and shook them gracefully.

"He always gets what he wants," another artist, who didn't get a license stood up angrily.

"Yes, I know, I've been very lucky," Super Man said gratefully.

"What about us? We didn't even get to draw a second draw!" Someone else slammed the door and left the restaurant.

The next day, the twenty-six artists went to City Hall to register their businesses, each paid a fee of four hundred dollars, and received a laminated vendor's license for the following year.

"There won't be any fights for better spots in the future," Super Man said. The licensed artists all had agreed that at the end of next August they would not renew their licenses automatically but meet again for another round of lots.

From the summer of 1989, when Big Brush and Ming started selling portrait art on the sidewalk of Yonge and Dundas, the portrait art market remained vibrant at the Eaton Centre location for a whole decade. It had drawn millions of tourists and residents to downtown Toronto long after Eaton Centre had filed for bankruptcy and Sears had bought up the Eaton empire.

Entering the twenty-first century, Sears renovated the old Eaton building and redesigned its front entrance. The new lobby stretched outwards onto the existing sidewalk, leaving only enough space for pedestrians to walk by and passengers to wait for streetcars. With the construction of Dundas Square across from the Sears building, downtown Toronto finally had a small public square for free concerts and other public events, imitating the spirit of Times Square in New York City. There was definitely no space for portrait artists to work at this intersection.

After leaving the busy downtown spot, the portrait market quickly died out. The artists dispersed to other cities. Ming decided to go to Europe with a few artist friends. In the following decade, she travelled from city to city in Europe, painting portraits of tourists and residents.

Within that decade, Big Brush and some of the other street artists qualified for the Guaranteed Income Supplement and the Old Age Security pension. Big Brush moved into a one-bedroom apartment in a government subsidized seniors' residence. Around Christmas each year, when Ming came back from Europe, she would call Big Brush and plan an outing to the Art Gallery of Ontario, so he could enjoy looking at his favourite postimpressionist artists, Paul Cézanne and Claude Monet. Later they would sit by Henry Moore's sculptures for an hour before going to their favourite International City Restaurant in Chinatown for Dim Sum. During the 2019 Christmas holidays, Big Brush invited Ming to his residence for their reunion.

It was New Year's Eve of 2019. Light snowflakes were silently falling in the early afternoon and rays of sunshine occasionally broke through the cloudy sky. Carrying a few food containers of takeout from their favourite restaurant, Ming stepped into Big Brush's apartment. She was immediately taken by surprise, experiencing a sense of dislocation. The one-bedroom seniors' apartment had been dramatically transformed into a working art studio.

In the middle of the living room, in front of the large window facing Lake Ontario, stood a workstation four by eight feet. The tabletop was covered with a well stained felt blanket typically used by Chinese brush-painting artists. On top of the workstation was a large stone inkwell, a few dinner plates used as palettes and completely stained, Chinese paint brushes of different sizes, tubes of water colour, and a small bucket of water. On the walls were framed and unframed paintings hung at different angles, some recent ones, displaying experimental calligraphies and landscape paintings, stuck on the wall with pushpins. In a corner of the room, away from the window, wrinkled original paintings were piled up on the floor.

"Are they your new works?" Ming asked.

"Oh, yes," Big Brush nodded, "Go take a look, and pick one you like."

Crouching in front of the pile of paintings, Ming flipped them one by one on the floor to get an idea of what the old artist had been doing. Big Brush had mixed Chinese art mediums with contemporary semiabstract styles to depict Canadian landscapes. From the stack, Ming picked up one that caught her eye immediately; the painting illustrated how the artist had made a far and wide departure from the traditional motif of plum flowers and landscape of Chinese brush paintings.

"Your work has changed dramatically," she commented.

"I need to communicate with contemporary audiences," answered Big Brush firmly. "You see, I don't need to worry about making a living any more. A stable government income every month, rain or shine or snow," he pointed at the window; outside, snowflakes continued to drift down steadily.

"In my remaining life," he began and paused, as he poured green tea from a blue-white porcelain teapot for his guest. "In my remaining life, I shall concentrate on one task only. That is to help Chinese brush painting, which is the oldest living art form in this world, enter the contemporary Canadian art field. If Western oil painting could be accepted in China a few decades after it was initially introduced, Chinese brush painting should have its opportunity to enter the Canadian art scenes."

Sipping hot green tea, Ming recalled that they had known each other for more than a decade and a half. While Big Brush's words rang familiarly in her ears, she said emotionally, "You haven't changed at all." In fact, Big Brush was talking about the same dream when they first met at the art gallery on Spadina and Dundas. "Do you remember the name of the art gallery, where we first met?"

"Art gallery? Which art gallery?" Big Brush replied.

Ming recalled to herself how she had visited the Chinese art gallery on the spur of a mysterious urge one spring day. But she couldn't recall why she had brought her old mother there to listen to Big Brush talk about his abiding dream.

Pouring more tea for them, Big Brush said, "Ming, I want to invite you to name the painting you have just picked from the pile."

"Oh? Are you sure, Brush?"

None of the paintings on the floor had been given a title yet, nor were they signed, dated, or ratified by the artist's personal seal. She was fully aware of the rare, lifetime honour for a younger artist being asked to name an old artist's painting. She felt emotionally loaded.

"I liked this painting immediately because of its mysterious mood. I like to think it is early spring because the tone is slightly warm and delicate, the motion is breezy, and the overwhelming mood is misty and mysterious." Ming paused before delivering her final thoughts, "What about 'Cherry Blossom Snow' for a title? It reminds me of the Japanese spring ritual called Sakura Hanami."

"Life's inevitable loss," the old artist concluded.

They sipped more tea. Ming came up with an alternative perspective. "However, considering the law of energy conservation, I have a semiabstract title for your semiabstract painting." She looked at Big Brush, expecting his encouragement.

"Oh, let's hear it, your semiabstract title," he said, standing up holding the teapot.

"Pink Energy Unfolds." Ming squeezed out the three words, then stopped.

Big Brush put down the teapot on the table. He asked Ming to repeat the title. When she did, he followed her to pronounce each word. "Mm, I just knew that I should show my paintings to the younger generation of artists."

Around midnight, the two artists bid good night and Happy New Year to each other at the final moment of 2019 and the first of 2020. Outside the seniors' residence, heavy snow had already covered up the 2019 footprints on the sidewalk. Ming was carrying the painting in an art tube across her shoulders, which was the New Year's gift from Big Brush to her. The old artist had inscribed both titles onto the painting, signed his name, dated it, and finally pressed down his personal seal in red.

Ming was walking against the wind to get to the subway station. While she was leaving a line of fresh footprints on the snow-covered sidewalk and street crossing, she didn't know this was the last time that she would visit Big Brush.

Around the same time in December 2019, the SARS-Coronavirus was breaking out from Wuhan, China. The virus was later officially named COVID-19 by the World Health Organization.

Another month later on March 11, 2020, WHO finally declared the global outbreak of COVID-19 a pandemic. By then this pandemic had spread out from Wuhan to the world. Wherever it landed, the initial mortalities were seniors in big cities living in group homes, long-term care facilities, and crowded neighbourhoods. Throughout the first six months of 2020, thousands of elderly persons died alone in total isolation without seeing their family members or friends. Big Brush was one of them.

Ming didn't return to Europe.

Under the Big Tree

A week before Christmas, I received a telephone call from an acquaintance of some years ago. I didn't remember his name, but I responded with a friendly familiarity just the same. Strangely, he didn't even detect my disguised embarrassment, concentrated as he was on making a holiday proposal. "I would like to invite you to dinner," he offered cheerfully, "to meet with a *da wan* [大腕] from China." After throwing in the trendy Chinese word, in the dramatic pause that followed, he waited for my response.

I had already heard this word, coined recently and now in wide circulation. *Da wan* referred to a new breed of Mainland Chinese, who had become extremely wealthy during the economic reforms of the late twentieth century. As a matter of fact, some *da wan*, both men and women, have already arrived in our cities, riding on the Millionaire Program offered by Immigration Canada. For better or for worse, these extremely rich Mainland Chinese had pushed up Canadian real estate markets, first in Vancouver and then in Toronto, sending feverish signals to the Bank of Canada to curb the overheated housing markets. Both the Ontario and British Columbia provincial governments had raised the land transfer taxes for residential real estate properties sold to non-resident buyers.

"Why should I be interested in meeting a *da wan* from China?" I asked.

"Because he is also an artist."

After the Christmas candles had long burned out, and giftwraps were crumpled into the recycle bins behind the houses, on a drizzling Monday evening I was driving into a mixed-zone area consisting of industry and business in Scarborough. The whole street block where I arrived was cloaked in a misty, gloomy atmosphere without streetlights. The low-rise, flat-roofed warehouse looked like a collection of solid cement blocks. "What a place to meet," I thought, turning my car intuitively toward the only window that had a light.

It was a photographer's studio. Behind the brightly-lit windowpane, a young bride dressed in a long, fluffy, white wedding gown was standing beside her groom in a white tuxedo. The young couple were posing for summer wedding photos in front of a large pull-down canvas background. As I was close enough to the building, I checked the unit next door illuminated by the light from the photographer's window. To my relief, it was Master Art Studio, where I was supposed to go. I parked the car on the opposite side of the road, tiptoed back through the slush and puddles on the ground. Gently, I knocked on the studio door.

A middle-aged man with shoulder-length hair opened the door. "Teacher Lee?" I greeted him in the Chinese custom of using a person's profession as part of the personal title.

"Hi, you must be Teacher Hu," Lee greeted me in the same fashion. "Thank you for coming to my humble studio." Bending slightly forward, he shook my hand politely.

Many Chinese artists in Toronto relied on teaching children

and other private students to make a decent living. Teacher Lee's art studio was furnished as a functional classroom with a line of pale florescent lights on the ceiling. In the central area there were four rectangular foldable tables arranged back to back to make two shared workstations. Eight foldable chairs were placed around each workstation. On the surrounding walls were displays of children's drawings made with colour pencils and crayons.

"Please feel free to look around," Lee pointed to the inner space, as if I were a parent coming to inspect and evaluate his art school. In the second classroom, the displays were obviously from students of higher grades, depicting still life, landscapes, portraits, and even some abstract compositions. They had used various art media, including pencil and charcoal for sketches, water colour for landscape, oil and acrylic for portraits, floral arrangements, and landscapes.

I heard Lee running to the door. "Hi, Teacher Lee, please meet our special guest Mr Shu, his pen name is Da Shu, Big Tree."

I already knew the excited, high-pitch voice belonging distinctively to Ray, who had called me two months ago to arrange for this special meeting. Shortly after his call that day, I recalled that Ray's Chinese name was Xiao Ri, meaning Morning Sun and that he was a mixed-media artist.

At this time a third man came in through the door. It was Tien He, an artist originally from Taiwan, whose Chinese name meant Milky Way. Tien He and I had known each other for more than a decade, as participants in many group exhibitions. I came to the lobby to greet Tien He with a friendly hug.

With one hand up, Ray raised his voice dramatically to introduce me to the special guest: "Master Shu, please meet our *mei nu* [美女] painter, Ms Hu."

I was quite shocked to hear Ray using the gender-sensitive modifier "beautiful female" in his introduction of me to another professional artist. However, at that moment I had no choice but to accept the unusual and unwanted flattery. I walked over to give our special guest a typical Chinese welcome with a warm handshake and, in addition, the usual Canadian greeting to an international guest, "Welcome to Canada."

Finally, we were all seated around the tables. Ray started the meeting with a brief speech. "It is a great honour for us in Toronto to meet with Mr Da Shu, Big Tree, who is known in China as the Supreme Master of Contemporary Chinese Art!"

We applauded warmly. Ray continued, "Master Shu would like to organize a contemporary Chinese artists' salon in Toronto. We would meet once a month to share our ideas and plan joint exhibitions in China and Canada. Any suggestions?" Ray looked at us around the table, and Lee raised his hand. "We look forward to exhibiting our artwork with Mr Big Tree. Now to best express our appreciation, please allow me to quote an ancient Chinese saying. 'Enjoy the shade under the big tree.'" While Lee's voice resonated in the air, we clapped again to welcome the founder of our new salon, who was smiling.

Ray looked around the table, "Any suggestions for exhibitions in Toronto or other cities in Canada?"

This time I picked up the ball. "In recent years, I have participated in the Asian Heritage Month annual art exhibitions. The nonprofit organization promotes Asian Canadian artists. Its venues are usually municipal government office buildings and public libraries. The exhibitions are guaranteed to be viewed by thousands of Canadians daily. If you guys are interested, I can certainly introduce our salon to the curator." I paused, looked around, and waited for a response. After a long minute, I only heard the humming of the florescent lights from the ceiling, as if enhancing my disappointment in the response to my suggestion.

Someone started to shift on the uncomfortable foldable metal chair. Ray's energetic voice broke through the silence. "OK, why don't I share with you my artistic adventure in C City just east of Toronto? Teacher Lee, I hope you won't mind hearing the same story more than once."

Lee shrugged his shoulders with a crooked smile, as if to say he had no choice.

On a beautiful Sunday afternoon last summer, Ray was walking past an art gallery inside a provincial park near his family cottage by Lake Ontario. A large crowd of well-groomed men and women were arriving for the opening reception of an art exhibition. Without giving it a second thought, Ray walked in as intensively as a small metal object flying toward a powerful magnet. Once inside the gallery, he started examining all the exhibits, one by one, from the paintings on the walls to the colourful paper sculptures hanging down from the ceiling. Then hoping to talk to someone, he crossed the floor to the information table opposite the entrance, where wine and cheese were being served. With great enthusiasm, Ray addressed the man and woman sitting behind the table.

"Hi, my name is Ray, I am a mixed-media artist living in C City. I really enjoyed your exhibition." The woman smiled at him and Ray continued, "Actually, I would very much like to join your group. I wonder if I can have an application form." To make himself at home, Ray picked up a copy of the current exhibition catalogue and a small plastic glass of white wine from the table.

"The catalogue and the wine are five dollars each. Ten dollars together, no taxes," the woman said flatly with a dry smile. "Of course, they are free for our members."

Searching his pocket, Ray pulled out a handful of quarters. He was embarrassed. With an awkward smile, he returned both the booklet and the wine to their places.

"I'm very sorry, I don't have my wallet with me right now, just came out for a walk." Ray felt even more inadequate when he realized he was in a T-shirt and shorts. "I'm truly sorry that I am not dressed for the occasion. I was walking by when I saw the exhibition poster outside, I just came in . . . . I am really glad I did though, because I have truly enjoyed the show."

Ray had a sincere urge to explain to the organizers that it was not for the wine or cheese that he had invited himself in. Alternatively, if he had a glass of wine in his hand, it would definitely make it easier for him to mingle with the club members. "If I could file a membership application today, that would be really great."

The woman asked her colleague sitting beside her, "John, do we have a membership application form?" John didn't answer, nor did he look at Ray standing in front of the table. But then suddenly he stood up and walked toward the gallery entrance to greet a middle-aged white couple that had just arrived.

Ray was stunned. Stepping back, he observed John from a distance as the latter was greeting the well-dressed couple, one by one, kissing the lady on the cheek, and then chatting with them there at the entrance. Looking around the gallery floor with a quick sweeping glance, Ray noticed for the first time that he was the only non-white person there. He understood now why his request for a membership application form had been ignored. For Ray the bright summer afternoon had suddenly changed into an icy winter night. Was this the multiracial and multicultural Canada he had been told about, where strangers smiled naturally at each other?

"Excuse me, Ray, for interrupting you," Tien He stood up indignantly. "You were an intruder, wearing T-shirt and shorts to an artists' club opening reception; how could you demand to join their club on the spot?"

Lee raised his eyebrows and nodded in agreement.

Ray looked irritated. He shifted his position noisily on the metal chair and replied loudly, "Why? You mean you don't know why?" He looked at all of us disappointedly. "Let me tell you why, because it was not right! I felt totally uncomfortable, out of place, to be exact, when I walked into an all-white artists' society. My sense as a Canadian was offended. Initially, I just wanted to join them because I liked their venue. Later, I felt I must join them to challenge their attitude."

We all remained silent, caught in a dilemma. We were not sure if we felt solidarity with Ray's position or consider him a shameless intruder for lacking basic professional respect for other artists' organization. Meanwhile our *da wan* guest remained quiet with great curiosity and concern on his face. A few minutes later, Ray spoke again, "As a result, I did join the organization the following week, and immediately signed up for the members' exhibition in the fall."

At this point, Lee stood up, saying, "Bravo! Bravo!" as did Tien He and I. Surprisingly, our *da wan* guest from China also joined us by clapping his hands. I believe Tien He and I cheered for the happy outcome rather than Ray's unreasonable, confrontational behaviour. Ray looked radiant and was reluctant to end his story. At a different time, we might have let him go on, but as it was getting late, we were all hungry and impatient. Suddenly, following Tien He, I also had an irresistible, intuitive urge to interrupt Ray.

"So at the exhibition last fall, did you give John your true Chinese colour see-see?" By translating *mot-a-mot* a Chinese idiom into English, I dumped a crazy babel of tongues. With this mini linguistic bomb, I couldn't suppress a string of laughter. While I was expecting the guys to follow suit, they didn't, except Ray, for the opposite effect. He looked like a fighting rooster with bloodshot eyes; obviously, he was not a bit amused by my epistemological playfulness, but rather upset at being disrupted for losing the continuity of his story.

"Stop! *Mei Nu*," he raised his index finger at me; without losing his total coolness, calling me "beautiful woman." I knew he could have called me some ugly names, such as "Banana," a popular racial slur, meaning white inside and yellow outside. I apologized to him for my badly timed joke.

At this moment, our cool *da wan* guest stood up from his chair for the first time in the evening. "Time to eat?" he asked politely, consulting us with his soft inquiring eyes, "before the restaurant closes."

We all agreed.

Outside the Master Art Studio, we noisily squeezed into our guest's Land Rover like a group of hungry kids. Whenever I felt hunger surging, I recalled my mother's timeless saying, "People regard food as heaven." According to her, food was at the essential core of Chinese culture. After I left China, I knew it being true for all cultures. The Land Rover made a few turns and stopped in a large parking lot. Through the foggy car window, suddenly I saw an indisputable endorsement of my mother's philosophy written on the front of the Chinese restaurant that was our destination.

"I can't believe this!" I exclaimed. "The restaurant is called People Regard Food as Heaven!"

Lee looked at me with an alarming expression on his face, "Didn't you know this place?"

"No, I didn't. What an amazing coincidence! I was just thinking about what my mother used to say. Her words are displayed in the name of the restaurant."

"You must be truly hungry," Lee said. He jumped down from the vehicle to hold the door open for me.

We walked into a large dining hall with traditional European décor: vaulted ceilings with hidden lights and dangling crystals from large chandeliers. On this cold Monday night, even this popular Hong Kong restaurant was nearly empty, with only two waitresses on duty. The guys walked toward a large round table for ten people in the furthest corner, making one of the waitresses run after us with a pile of embossed leather menus.

"Peking Duck served in two ways, Dong Po pork, large West Lake beef egg-drop soup, Singapore fried noodles . . . " The names of well-known traditional Chinese dishes spilled from the lips of fellow artists without opening the menus in their hands.

"Anything else?" They looked at me. From the menu, I picked a dish called Three Kinds of Mushrooms with *Jie Lan* [芥蘭]. I decided not to mention that I am, most of the time, a vegetarian, and that half of the food I eat daily are vegetables. My diet had gradually evolved to be such, which was a far and wide departure from traditional Chinese cuisine. However, whenever I had a chance to go out with friends, I would eat almost everything on the table, especially if there was Peking Duck.

Shortly after our order was taken into the kitchen, a middle-aged chef in a white uniform, white chef's cap, and a red scarf around his neck pushed a trolley out of the kitchen toward our table. Sitting on a large silver plate on top of the trolley was a golden-brown Peking duck. As Chinese, we likely knew the chef would shave the crispy duck in front of our eyes if it was not already prepared inside the kitchen. Assuming that most of us probably had opportunities to watch this performance some-where before, none of us said anything, we simply continued with our conversation.

The chef must have noticed our indifference toward his arrival. He made no fuss about his special presentation for customers who had ordered a whole duck. Rather than arousing our interest and appetite to watch him, he quietly made a start and completed the job without calling for our attention. When he placed two plates of duck slices on the table, our taste buds were eventually aroused by the aroma of the crispy duck skin.

I accidentally caught the chef's last look before he headed back to the kitchen; I saw a flare of emotional distress as he placed the knife on the lower level of the trolley. At that moment, I remembered seeing his photo at the entrance of the restaurant. Few customers cared to know that he was an Iron Chef, a winner of the famous cooking competition in Hong Kong. I was truly embarrassed by our untutored behaviour toward the Iron Chef, who regarded food presentation as we did our paintings and sculptures in the art galleries.

"Thank you very much for your excellent presentation." An acknowledgement of gratitude rushed from my lips, but it was too late to save the situation when I heard a deep sigh from the chef. He nodded at me with an apologetic smile, before pushing the trolley back into the kitchen, his eyes cast low.

As we started enjoying the savory food, our conversation naturally touched upon no other subjects but food. Tien He said his favourite Peking Duck restaurant was the original Qian Ju De Peking Duck in downtown Beijing, not too far from Tiananmen Square. I said mine would have to be the Duck King near the Olympic Stadium. As I saw our guest Da Shu nodding at me, I decided to share an unforgettable experience with the group.

Duck King entertained guests who bought a VIP package. Before the performing chef entered the private dining room, a waitress would formally announce the chef's name just as at any performance on stage. The audience were invited to participate by counting the number of the duck slices once the chef started to perform. After the introduction, the chef came in with a shining Peking duck sitting on a tray. In the next ten minutes, the guests focused all their attention on the chef's deft movements as if watching a magician on the stage. As they counted, a slice of the crispy duck fell into the designer white dish which had a long-neck duck head. The duck slices arranged themselves formally as they flew in, piece by piece, directed by the dancing movements of the chef's knife. When the count reached one hundred and eight, the chef stopped, showing off a bony duck skeleton completely shaved. The guests, their jaws dropping, stood up to give the chef a heartfelt applause and a standing ovation. No one would forget this unique scene.

"But tonight," I sighed, "how many of us have even noticed that the chef was performing for us?" The guys looked at each other and shrugged their shoulders. They couldn't recall what had happened half an hour before the two plates of duck slices were placed in front of them.

"Thank you! Thank you very much, *Mei Nu*!" With his loud dramatic voice, Ray stood up, helping the waitress who had come to deliver two more hot dishes to our table. I started to appreciate how Ray greeted every woman equally with the same cliché, *Mei Nu*, beautiful woman. All the women who were being flattered tonight, myself included, gave Ray a grateful or modest smile in return. I no longer wondered why none of the women were upset when Ray used the same cliché toward us. On the contrary, referring all of us to a category of physical beauty seemed to connect well with the deep psychological code imbedded originally in our beings.

Nourished by the heavenly food for more than an hour, I noticed the mood of the group had improved greatly. While *Pu Er* tea [普洱茶] was being poured, the conversation around the table had become less combative, more relaxing and comforting. "Da Shu," Lee started to address our *da wan* guest with his pen name. "Thank you for organizing the salon, we will be looking forward to working with you in the near future."

"Apparently," said Ray, taking the opportunity to promote our guest, "Da Shu's Chinese brush paintings and calligraphies are among the most sought-after items by collectors in the Chinese art market. You guys may have heard that one of his paintings had an offer of 20,000,000 yuan, about 3,300,000 Canadian dollars back then, from a Taiwanese collector, but he donated the painting to the 2008 Beijing Olympic Games."

We looked at Da Shu in disbelief. "What did you depict in the painting?" I asked curiously, "And what's the title of the painting?"

"The title is *Zhong guo ren ming le qi lai le!*" Da Shu answered word by word, as if we might not be able to catch each word.

"In English, *Chinese People Are Laughing!*" Ray added.

I was in Beijing during the 2008 Olympic Games and my family had watched the events on TV every day. All of a sudden, I recalled the opening ceremony directed by Chinese movie director Zhang Yimou, which actually started with an initial scene of unrolling a traditional long scroll of Chinese brush painting. I stared at Da Shu, did he actually create the long scroll? What an unusual title! How did he compose it for such a title? I would have loved to see a digital image of the painting, *Chinese People Are Laughing!*

Clearing his throat, Da Shu explained, "I chose this title as a parallel to match Chairman Mao's historical announcement. The world will never forget the powerful statement made by Chairman Mao on top of the Tiananmen Platform. 'The Chinese people are standing up!'" Da Shu's eyes shone with sparks reflecting the dangling crystals of the chandeliers.

I held my breath until he finished his explanation. How dare he claim that he had created the title to match Chairman Mao's historical speech? Did he forget numerous political movements in Mainland China since 1949? Thousands of innocent people were persecuted to death for careless remarks indirectly referring to Mao or the Communist Party.

I couldn't believe that Da Shu could simply get away without dire consequences after saying such a politically incorrect title out aloud. Meanwhile he switched his topic to Deng Xiaoping's Economic Reform.

"Since China is now a world economic powerhouse, my title, *Chinese People Are Laughing!* depicts the simple fact that Chinese all over the world, including overseas Chinese and the Chinese diaspora, shouldn't you be proud of your Chinese heritage?" Da Shu's face was turning red after a few drinks. As overseas Chinese, we all agreed with him. Although our daily life was only marginally related to China's booming economy, we were truly happy to see a more prosperous China. Mainland Chinese could now apply for their passports and travel in the world for the first time since 1949.

The lights overhead dimmed and turned back on, and we realized the restaurant was about to close. Ray gestured to a waitress and she brought the bill folder. Da Shu immediately pulled out a small stack of one-hundred-dollar bills from his wallet but the rest of us also offered to share the expense.

"Please allow me the privilege of paying for the dinner," Da Shu said graciously. "Money is not a problem for me." His sincerity made us feel comfortable to put away our wallets.

"Master Shu, thank you very much for the lovely dinner," said I. Lee followed me immediately, "We appreciate the shade under the Big Tree." Then Tien He stood up with the traditional Chinese body language of *bao quan* [抱拳]. With his left hand touching his right hand in a fist, placing both hands in front of his chest, he expressed his gratitude to the master guest and his fellow artists. *Bao quan* was widely adopted by martial artists from ancient times to the contemporary era.

Outside the restaurant, the rain had stopped. A clear new moon was half way up in the starless night sky. Da Shu's Land Rover was the only vehicle remaining in the parking lot. With the cool night air clearing our minds, instead of calling off this Monday evening meeting before midnight, we all agreed to go back to Lee's studio for more tea.

I was still hoping to see the image of Da Shu's famous painting, *Chinese People Are Laughing!*

Back in the Master Art Studio, we felt a companionship that hadn't existed before. The humming noise from the florescent lights seemed less intrusive than before. And Lee no longer hesitated to bring out his treasured English tea set of delicate cups with matching saucers.

My mind was still preoccupied by the English translation of the title of Da Shu's painting, *Chinese People Are Laughing!* The word, *laughing*, suggested an uncontrollable burst of emotion in an audible vocal convulsion, but that was not what the original Chinese title implied. The phrase in the Chinese title, *le qi lai le*, based on colloquial northern Chinese, was tricky to translate. The word *le* relates to happiness, which when used as a verb, could mean laugh happily with or without sound, likely not a convulsion, more like giggle, grin, or titter. However, these English synonyms may also imply something else, which the more innocent Chinese verb *le* does not possess. I asked myself, how about "Chinese People Are Smiling!" *Smiling* implies a silent facial muscle movement, a coy smile, as in Leonardo da Vinci's portrait of *Mona Lisa*, which probably does not need an exclamation mark! How about "Chinese People Are Happy (or Happier)." Without an action verb, the title would not match the syntax of Chairman Mao's original phrase, and so it would dull the impact of the artist's original rather risky statement.

Through the night I felt burdened by an obligation to come up with a better title for Da Shu. If the painter had adopted a different title, such as "Chinese People Are Smiling" or "Chinese People Are Happy!" that might save his life one day. In China or Canada,

I had never met or heard about anyone who was so naïve, ignorant, pig-headed, or egotistical as he was. If there were another widespread purge in China of potential discontented intellectuals or egotistic artists, Da Shu would likely be accused of committing a serious crime. Since he had openly declared that the title he had created purposely matched Chairman Mao's famous phrase, delivered in Mao's thick Hunan accent on September 21, 1949, Da Shu would never be able to deny or repudiate his original intention. If history repeated itself, which had happened many times in China, including during the decades after 1949, Da Shu, the enemy of the Chinese people would deserve to die a thousand times in the public square in Beijing.

"Hey, old buddy, are you going to help us get rich?" said Ray brashly, as if the salon members were now demanding something more after the grand dinner they were treated to by the guest. The rest of us, quietly sipping tea, were startled. We stared at Ray, waiting to see the effect. As Ray had called Da Shu Old Buddy so casually, we began to wonder whether we had been potentially connected with the latter's business network in Mainland China. After all, he was the founder of our new salon.

We were expecting Ray to invite the guest to share with us his artistic journey that had eventually led him to win the title of Superior Master of Contemporary Chinese Art. Instead, Ray had made a childish demand, showing an undisguised envy for Da Shu's wealth. Now we felt sorry for Da Shu, his fancy, glorious feathers had been carelessly stripped off before we had a chance to appreciate their full colours. What would Da Shu think of Chinese Canadian artists after meeting with us?

Da Shu smiled. He looked quite content, sitting across the table from me. Without hesitation or pretentious modesty, he responded to Ray's invitation naturally and professionally. "As far as I know, there is no get-rich-fast formula. However, having said that, I do believe there are smart, effective formulas in all disciplines, including the field of fine arts. You need to find your own smart, effective formula and stick to it, and in the long run it will likely lead you to success."

He stopped right there, waiting for our response.

Lee stood up. He announced cheerfully as if he were the MC now, "Let's warmly welcome Da Shu, head of our new salon, to share with us his personal formula for success! After all, we are gathering under the shade of the Big Tree." He chuckled, looking at us, and we joined him in another applause.

Da Shu beamed agreeably, "Sure, sure, now I will 'open the door for you to see the mountains.'" He burst out laughing, having quoted another old Chinese saying. Ray drummed on the table with his fingers, Tien He and I clapped our hands in the background. Da Shu continued, "Before I knew there might be a potential personal path to success somewhere, I realized that I must investigate the Chinese art markets. I followed ancient Chinese wisdom, some of the known strategies written by Sunzi [孫子] in his famous book, The Art of War [孫子兵法]. Sunzi advised that knowing yourself and knowing your opponents, you would not lose one out of a hundred battles. Now I want to ask you, have any of you been to the higher-end art auctions in China?"

The men looked at each other, shaking their heads, "No, no, not yet."

"I have, Master Shu, in Beijing," I said.

"That's great! Can you tell us the types of merchandise you saw at the art auctions?"

I hesitated, feeling somewhat uncomfortable about the word "merchandise," since we were really talking about original artwork, not commercial reproductions such as T-shirts, tote bags, postcards, cups and books.

After a couple of seconds, Da Shu explained, "Basically, there should be two large categories of art merchandise: First, dead masters' works from different historical periods. They rarely exist in contemporary Chinese art markets or even with private collectors." Da Shu recalled that the most horrendous destruction of dead Chinese art masters' works had happened during the Proletarian Cultural Revolution started in 1966, which had the mission to wipe out all feudal cultural products and influences. A nationwide campaign was launched to search for cultural pieces and antiques from private homes; they were confiscated by the government. Years later they were massively sold by China in overseas markets in exchange for foreign currencies that China desperately needed during the 1970s and 1980s. Our guest let out a deep sigh.

After sipping some tea, Da Shu continued, "Therefore what are called dead masters in Chinese art markets today are actually artists of the early to mid-twentieth century." The artworks of the modern period were obtained as gifts directly from the artists themselves or purchased by investors and collectors from the artists' families or other sources. With these possessions, following the Economic Reforms of the mid-1990s, art investors had created the profit-driven Chinese art market. Later some national powerhouses got involved, such as the military Poly Group, and the Chinese art market grew rapidly. The Poly Group organized large art auctions in Beijing, Guangzhou, and Shanghai. With the dead masters' original pieces selling at accelerating prices, fine art suddenly became a powerful commodity for Chinese investors. The powerhouse *da wan* investors have led the art market to where it is today, and they will continue to drive the art market in the future.

As soon as Da Shu had finished, Lee raised a question. "What is the second largest category of merchandise in the Chinese art market today?"

"Indeed, what is it? That's a very good question." Da Shu acknowledged Lee's clever question with a smile. "In fact, what had caught my attention ten years ago was the second group." He paused, gathering all our attention at the table before resuming, "I noticed that what had physically filled up the art auctions were excellent and mediocre paintings and calligraphies by contemporary artists. I could foresee that in the future, some of the contemporary artists would be the future masters. It was right there, ten years ago, I saw a potential opportunity for me to enter the Chinese art market." Da Shu paused for a second, "Do you see my point? A potential entrance into the Chinese art market!" Saying which he leaned back in his chair.

The first time Da Shu said "*da wan*," referring to art investors, we nearly burst out laughing. After he had repeatedly used the slang, it didn't sound funny or awkward to our ears any more. Meanwhile, we could see how the powerhouse groups in China through the centralized political and financial systems controlled, manipulated, and grabbed the huge resources of ordinary Chinese people. Once possessed by the elite investors, the dead Chinese art masters' paintings had immediately become high-profit commodities at the international art auctions.

Da Shu picked up his tea cup; we watched him gently blow the floating tea leaves to the edges of the cup, before taking a sip. He didn't swallow it immediately, but held it for a few seconds before letting it slowly and silently go down his throat. He paused again before taking another sip.

I saw bright smiles in his eyes.

I could recall some art auctions in Beijing. They were held in luxury hotels along Subway Line One in the CBD area, the most prosperous part of the national capital. During viewing days, spectators would swarm the hotel lobby. Many were retirees or serious art lovers who had some knowledge of Chinese art. Some of them were potential buyers, though it would be rare for them to compete in a bidding war. They came with auction catalogues and equipped with iPads or other electronic devices. Wearing comfortable cotton outfits and athletic walking shoes, they came prepared to examine the displays lane by lane, area by area, tirelessly working their way through the labyrinth of paintings. With no anxiety to rush through the maze quickly, these individual speculators lingered in front of the paintings, jotting down notes in the catalogue. As a small group, they sat down somewhere on a bench, sharing information in secretive whispers to avoid disturbing other visitors.

From time to time I tried to eavesdrop on this type of speculator by staying in the same lane or behind the paintings in the next lane, perking up my ears like a rabbit. I was curious about what knowledgeable art lovers and speculators were interested in. But I had never run into a *da wan* buyer in the exhibition area. After visiting several large art auctions in Beijing, I concluded that art investors, who likely could purchase an artist's entire portfolio at bargain price before the auction day, only listened to the market analysis prepared exclusively for them by an art investment adviser. I imagined this scene only existed behind the closed doors of the VIP lounges, where wine, food, and exquisite tea services with delicate finger desserts were offered to the guests at any time.

According to the auction results, *da wan* buyers and art investors would eventually move half of the artwork registered for each auction, having negotiated their deals before sending in an agent on the auction day. Qualified individual artists, who planned to enter the commercial art market for the first time, were given a price range they could list with the condition that they must preregister a confirmed buyer, who would definitely show up to purchase the artwork on the auction day. If these artists had loyal buyers they could build up their own network of collectors. Among the established artists, if some failed to find loyal customers, their names would disappear in the annual meteor shower of falling artists from the artistic sky dome. Auction companies likely would resell their artworks to new investors in the future.

In conclusion, I shared with my fellow artists at the table that we should not be surprised that the high-end Chinese art market, just like the real estate and stock markets, are controlled by the children and grandchildren of the politically powerful members, a special elite class related directly to current and past Communist Party leaders. I remembered to add a final reminder: "In any case, please don't let my observation spoil your expectation. Do your own diligent research and investigation."

As soon as I completed my report on the art auctions in Beijing, Da Shu and Tien He stood up and walked toward the washroom.

Ray and I remained sitting around the table, while Lee came around with the kettle to refill our teacups with hot water for the third time. Ray let out a deep sigh, leaning back and forth against his squeaking chair.

"Exactly," he uttered, as if picking up the thread of my comments. I wondered what he was thinking. After all, he had put our *da wan* guest on the spot, asking him how to get rich fast. After an entire hour spent on the subject, none of us knew anything about his secret to success. Suddenly Ray burst out with another totally unexpected topic. "As far as I can see, Chinese ink-wash painting is dead!" His dramatic announcement turned our heads. "No matter what you try to do, pouring ink, pouring colour, pouring water, semiabstract, abstract, Chinese ink-wash painting remains dead."

"Ah, for God's sake! Where did you get such rage? Do you know Chinese brush painting is the only living art form in the world, that has remained undisrupted from ancient times? Why do you want to place a death curse on its longevity?" Tien He sneered at Ray as he came back to the table.

"Why not?" Ray responded, snarling.

"Oh, a Chinese Nietzsche here, everyone!" Tien He announced sarcastically.

Lee joined in, "As the Chinese Nietzsche, Ray, you forgot to say that you have killed Chinese ink-wash painting just as Nietzsche said that his generation had 'killed God.'"

"Do you know what kind of crime it is to kill the world's oldest living art form? It's the murder of all murders!"

Tien He denounced Ray in the most condemnatory tone that we had ever heard him use.

"According to Nietzsche, there is no water that can clean the blood off our hands for committing such a crime?" I added more fuel to the fire.

Now Ray turned around to confront me, causing another series of squeaking noises from his chair. "You are right! *Mei Nu*, I seriously meant to say that we have killed Chinese brush painting, because after imitating the Chinese masters who were dead for thousands of years, we tried to imitate dead European masters in Chinese art. You cannot use a dead corpse to revive another dead corpse, it's as simple as that! That's exactly how we managed to kill Chinese brush painting." Ray threw a cold look at the rest of us. "This was the reason why I had stopped painting in Chinese art media for two years until I joined the white artists' club."

"Eh, that's very interesting! Just how did the white artists' club revive your interest in the dead-corpse of Chinese brush painting?" Tien He asked, emotionally and uncompromisingly.

Instead of shouting back, Ray raised his voice to stop us. "I've stopped mixing Chinese art media with western art form in my paintings, in order to prevent the uniqueness of the oldest living

art form being assimilated." He was busy searching his iPad, pushing buttons to flip multiple pages. Then, he passed his iPad to me,
"Please take a look at my new painting for the club's group exhibition last fall."

The image was an oil painting on a vertical rectangular canvas.
The artist had depicted a naked male torso with a shaved head
turned upwards, his neck stretched with bulging veins, and a
firmly set jaw. The arms and hands of the torso were tied down,
gracefully, by fluffy ribbons rather than ropes or chains. The ribbons wrapping the chest displayed a style similar to that of an
Egyptian mummy, except for the long loose ends dropping down
from the chest, occupying the entire foreground of the painting.
On the loosely hanging ribbons were characters expressing traditional Chinese values, covering a long twisting list from social and
cultural values to hierarchy, mannerisms, morality, loyalty, piety,
responsibility, longevity and so on. The characters were written
in various Chinese calligraphy styles as found on tortoise shells,
Li, Yan, Liu, and scripts—all in black tempera against the white
background of the canvas.

While the iPad was passed around the table, we became silent,
visually stimulated and mesmerized by the depiction in the
painting.

Eventually, it was Ray who broke the silence. "Remember
John? The white man who was reluctant to give me a membership application?" I let out a deep sigh that I had been holding for
some time. Ray had managed to resume his narrative from exactly
where he was interrupted before we went out for dinner. "At the
opening reception of the group exhibition, John came up to shake
my hand, asking for a picture with me in front of this painting."

"Is that why you wanted so badly to join them? Is that the
point?" Tien He uttered another scornful jibe at Ray. I also felt
disappointed in Ray's low expectation.

UNDER THE BIG TREE 55

"What's wrong with that?" Ray threw back a sharp look, "You guys still don't see the point, do you? For me to join them, first of all, made them acknowledge Canada included more than Caucasian Canadians, and second, I wanted to give them a chance to look at my work with respect."

"Ray, didn't you join the club last summer as you had wished? And didn't you enroll immediately in the exhibition for the fall show?" Tien He asked two rhetorical questions in a row.

"Yes, I did," answered Ray, looking confused, "what's your problem?"

"I have a problem with your attitude," Tien He said seriously. "As a Canadian artist, you are expected to follow the same professional regulations for all artists when applying for membership, artist grants, and exhibition opportunities. You need to stop shooting every issue with antiracism bullets. Your attitude, in fact, shows that you regularly discriminated against yourself and other minority members in society; from time to time, you openly demand racial minority privileges above the general regulations for all artists."

"Well said, Tien He!" Lee and I struck the table in loud support.

"Although confrontation is a good motivation for artistic creativity," Tien He added, "it doesn't equal to art." We agreed with him, although any form of cultural resistance and social rebellion, including civil disobedience and violent protest could be utilized for artistic creation.

However, Ray hadn't created outright confrontational propaganda to combat racism. Contrary to his own declarations, in front of our eyes, was a piece of art depicting a soul-searching process pursued by the artist in his new social and cultural environment. The Chinese cultural heritage which had formed the foundation of our imagination, paradoxically, could also become the bonds that constrained our imagination.

A collector had wanted to buy Ray's painting at the opening reception, but he declined the offer. "This painting," he said, "will never be placed for sale, because it records a personal and artistic journey that I have yet to complete. Like a caterpillar hanging down from a tree, I still need to wrap myself up in a pupa. It will take some more transformation before I can emerge a butterfly with pretty wings." A rare shy smile appeared on Ray's face. For the first time that evening, his speech had gone from confrontational to self-reflective.

The florescent lights above our heads became brighter as the night wore on. We heard the photographers next door saying their goodbyes and locking their door. Darkness and tranquility had descended on the compound outside. We were the only sleepless night owls, waiting for something to happen.

All this time, while we were talking about Ray's painting, Da Shu hadn't made a single comment, nor did his face change expression from the smile on his lips. Sitting on the opposite side of the table, I had the opportunity to observe him as he was listening attentively. My admiration had grown for this man's well reserved calm, showing no obvious signs of anxiety. Perhaps he had already completed his metamorphosis from a caterpillar to a butterfly with beautiful wings. Sitting among the caterpillars, he was fully aware that we were waiting for him to deliver his successful strategy about the Chinese art market.

"Sorry, I have taken too much of your time," Ray apologized to Da Shu. Tien He started to yawn. I covered my yawn and Lee stood up to stretch.

"Master Da Shu, the rest of the night is yours," announced Ray politely. "Are you going to teach us your formula for success?" This was the third time in the evening that Ray had invited the guest to disclose his secret of success.

When we had all sat down again at the table, Da Shu came straight to the point. "The discussion tonight is interesting. To me, there are two most important questions that each artist must ask yourself and seek answers to." His first question: What's the purpose of your artistic creation? Do you have an audience? The second question: If you have an audience, do you have potential buyers among them? Da Shu paused, his soft eyes gently swept across the table.

After a long pause, Tien He said that from the beginning of his artistic career, he had no idea what exactly the market meant to him. If he wanted to become a businessman, he said with a wry grin, he could have inherited his father's import-export business in Taiwan. Lee confessed that he had rented this studio eight years ago when his family first landed in Canada. The original purpose was to teach other people's kids so that his family could be fed. The goal was never to find an audience and buyers for his paintings. Eight years later, his family lived in a decent detached house, his two children had both entered universities, and he had emerged a reputable after-school art teacher in the Scarborough area.

"A success or a failure?" Lee asked us with a crooked smile.

A long silence prevailed in the room again, as we had no clear answer. What is success? and what is failure in life? I asked myself silently. A piece of ancient wisdom flashed in my mind from Lao Tzu who lived around 500 BCE. He said both success and failure were unstable conditions like standing on a ladder. Therefore, the passage of life could not possibly be like the unrolling of a long scroll of Chinese brush painting with ideally patterned motifs.

Ray let out a deep audible sigh. "For the two years when I didn't paint," he said, "I was depressed to see that many artists had spent their entire lives trying to enter the commercial art market. From time to time, I thought about jumping off a cliff along with the market to commit a double suicide if I could save art." Ray's pitiful dramatic confession somehow sent cold chills up our spines. How could anyone kill the commercial art market with a murder-suicide?

"Stop!" Da Shu brought his hand firmly on the table. "Stop talking nonsense! I am here to help you clear the confusion in your heads." He then continued in a much softer voice and said that art is always embedded with the purpose to serve the dominant hierarchy and to reinforce its social order. The numerous paintings in the Louvre depicting Biblical stories serve the Christian churches. However, across China in all the museums, you won't find a single painting depicting Mary and baby Jesus. Instead, the paintings focus on the history of the Chinese Communist Party and its leaders. All representational art helps to establish and strengthen the prevailing political, religious, and other social orders. Paintings in the museums display the winners and the dominant cultures of history.

Looking each of us in the eye in turn, Da Shu announced that now he would share with us his most important advice to artists: "Working with the market is the only way for artists to survive and thrive."

I looked at my watch to check the time: it was exactly midnight. If there were a grandfather clock in the room, we would have heard the pendulum striking twelve times, amplifying the moment as a turning point for our artistic vision for the future. But if we missed this particular midnight enlightenment, we would simply have finished waiting all night in vain. Whatever ideas that had sparkled throughout the night would simply be absorbed back into the universe when the transition between *Yin* and *Yang* energy reached equilibrium before dawn.

Da Shu continued, "I chose art to build bridges among people. Instead of being narcissistic or confrontational, I paint what people want to see."

Tien He raised his eyebrows, "Are you telling us that you try to please the market?"

"Yes and no," Da Shu said shrewdly with a smile, "if you follow the political events, or simply the news, it should not take you long to find out what the core of the nation is talking about. Once you know the national interest, you should focus your art on the same topic. Art buyers, who invest money in the costly merchandise, are usually successful people. Their decision to purchase a piece of artwork from a living artist is based on many factors, but not an obligation to flatter the artist. Therefore, it's your responsibility as an artist to find out what the successful clients and potential buyers want to see in the paintings." Da Shu paused, searching for agreement. I had no idea if we could comprehend the essence of his message. Was he saying that contemporary artists should go back to serving the national interest and government agenda?

Trying to keep our sleepy eyes open, we were puzzled and bewildered. None of us wanted to open another debate about propaganda art in modern Chinese history, such as the art of the Cultural Revolution. My generation grew up with propaganda art on the streets and in all media publications exclusively, which had an audience consisting of the entire nation. The artistic authenticity of the propaganda art had no significance for the artists, who only desired to serve the political power of the day. The artists often remained anonymous.

"To me, the true value of art begins when it is viewed," Ray uttered another ambivalent statement. I had an urge to remind him of the not-for-profit exhibitions I had suggested at the beginning of our meeting, which guaranteed a large audience but not a single sale. However, I was too tired to jump on him. In no time, Ray changed his own statement, "Of course, when buyers are willing to pay a large sum of money for a piece of authentic painting, art suddenly becomes a precious commodity for investors, just like gold and silver in the financial market."

"That's right!" exclaimed Da Shu excitedly, striking the table with both his hands at the same time. Standing up from his chair, he almost shouted, "Well said! Xiao Ri, finally you understood it!"

His dramatic action instantly aroused the rest of us. We also just realized that Da Shu only knew Ray's Chinese name.

"Xiao Ri, you've just stated the final point that I wanted to share with you all!" Da Shu continued. "Make your paintings into precious commodities for the collectors!" Now Da Shu looked exuberant as his message had finally gotten through to one thick head in the group. "Xiao Ri, now tell your friends about the title I have suggested for you!"

"Sure, I will," answered Ray, acknowledging a new special relationship between him and Da Shu. Picking up his teacup, Ray took a large mouthful and swallowed it noisily. We also heard his deep breathing, inhaling and exhaling. Finally, when he was ready to share the different story about him and Da Shu, his voice was soft. "Da Shu gave me a title a month ago after we first met. The deal is, if I could create a painting that deserves his title, he guarantees to sell the painting to one of his collectors for several million yuan. Of course, he may have to cosign the painting with me," Ray chuckled.

"What's the title?" Lee asked.

"It is called—are you ready?" Ray teased us again with his annoying habit of dramatizing anything. "The selling title is, 'White Cats and Black Cats.'" He spoke the words in a long descending tone, raising his hands then slowly lowering them. We burst into convulsive laughter, making the chairs squeak together, as if all the instruments in a symphony orchestra were reaching a crescendo, with Ray as the conductor.

Da Shu, our salon founder, sitting there with his sustained calm and reserve all night, didn't even smile at our collective response. "What are you laughing at?" he asked, looking quite upset. "'White Cats and Black Cats' is an established, famous phrase for a selling title. Over 1.4 billion Mainland Chinese understand it, so do overseas Chinese in business and finance. I have no doubt that the painting will sell at a great price."

At this stage, we could only vaguely remember Chinese leader Deng Xiaoping once saying something funny about cats. While we looked in embarrassment at each other, Ray reminded us, "Deng Xiaoping said, 'White cat, black cat, so long as it catches a mouse, it is a good cat.'"

Lee nodded at Da Shu, giving him a thumbs-up and Da Shu looked appeased. The great Chinese leader had used a simple metaphor that all Mainland Chinese could understand, and there was really nothing for us to laugh at. Perhaps we should be grateful to Da Shu, I thought, for teaching us how to find business opportunities. God had sent Big Tree to us, why didn't we just relax in the shade of his influence and connections in the Chinese art market?

Da Shu was comfortably leaning back on his foldable chair now. Occasionally, he nodded at us with approval and encouragement. Tien He asked Ray, "Have you given any serious thought to the composition?" We were all curious about how Ray planned to handle the broad implication of the title. The opportunity belonged to him alone unless he was willing to share it with us. Suddenly we were aware of potential legal issues. We had all heard the title tonight, but we should not attempt to steal it from Da Shu or Ray.

"How much time are you giving Xiao Ri to produce this painting?" Lee asked, showing a full awareness of Da Shu's reserved right to the painting under his title.

"Three months," answered Da Shu firmly, "to make some serious endeavour."

"Could it be a joint project for all of us at the first salon meeting tonight?" Lee continued boldly. "After all, with a few more cats, black and white, male and female, we can catch more mice." I was surprised that none of us laughed this time, as Lee had raised a difficult question on behalf of the salon collective. A long pause, the master painter kept his head straight and his mouth shut without granting an alternative chance for a potential collaboration.

In the end he said, "If Xiao Ri fails to make some serious effort within three months, I shall do it myself."

With Da Shu's final words, we suffered the disappointment in solid silence. It suddenly dawned on me what this master artist from China had tried to teach us. By rejecting Lee's request for us to share in the business opportunity, he had finally revealed the secret formula of his personal success. It was this, that the artist is responsible for his or her own artistic vision; they should find their own subject, execute the work themselves, and control the sale.

Ray had been invited to share Big Tree's potential personal collectors. It was a benevolent and friendly gesture from Big Tree toward a young artist. We should salute him for his kindness rather than demand it for ourselves. I continued the dialogue with myself in quiet contemplation until I heard hands clapping. I shook myself awake. As the co-chair of the salon, Ray had just finished his thank-you speech and proclaimed the end of the first salon meeting. As I got up with the others, I wondered if Ray had announced the date for the next salon gathering. I likely had missed it.

Outside the studio, crossing the road to my car, I felt my whole body being wrapped within the mysteries of an early dawn. Drops of cool morning dew were rolling down from my hair to my face, some landed on my eyelashes, some rolled into my mouth, some fell to the ground. In the stillness surrounding me at this hour when I was rarely awake, I began to feel a greater awareness. I heard the soft breath of seeds and worms in the soil; I felt the rustling of roots under my feet waiting patiently for their time to emerge when they would turn the world green. On the far horizon, the rising sun was about to break through a grey sky. The *yin/yang* cycle was progressing from night to day, and all lives would be infused with new energy.

Five W and H

Prologue: Where We Live

"What do you call a baby swan?" I asked my friend Wendy on the phone, "Is it a gosling or an ugly duckling?"

"No, no, a gosling is a baby goose," said Wendy with a smile in her voice, as if talking to her junior-high students before her retirement. "Baby swans are called cygnets. When they first emerge into life, they have short necks and thick down, so sometimes they are referred to as ugly ducklings. However, swans, geese, and ducks belong to the same water bird family called anatidae." Wendy, a retired natural science teacher, finished her precise answer to my casual question.

"Guess what, I saw some ducklings, maybe cygnets, swimming in the Ash Bridges Bay today! According to an ancient Chinese poet, ducks, ducklings, and maybe cygnets know spring before other species."

"Interesting, but how is that possible?" she replied.

Without further hesitation, I dropped a line from poet Su Shi [蘇軾] who lived one thousand years ago. "'Ducks know spring when the river feels slightly warm.' In Chinese, it sounds like this, '*chun jiang shui nuan ya xian zhi*'" [春江水暖鸭先知].

As an immigrant from Yorkshire, England, Wendy most likely wouldn't know the Song Dynasty Chinese poet, but her response surprised me. "That sounds like field notes, the poet must have observed ducks and ducklings on the river," she said. The high marks she gave to Su Shi's observation delighted me and we ended our conversation happily for sharing an intuitive joy of an early spring as creatures in the natural world. For the rest of the afternoon, I continued to feel energized by images of ducklings and cygnets swimming.

In the early evening, as a misty blue twilight was descending, I heard the footsteps of spring approaching. I listened to its movement, the rhythm of its breath, and the speed of its progress. I wondered if this was a poetic inspiration or the return of an old acquaintance. Suddenly, the doorbell rang, announcing a twilight messenger at my doorstep.

Who: A Spring Messenger

My friend, Holly, was the twilight messenger. A few days later we were driving to Richmond Hill, where Holly guided me to a two-story brick building. I parked in the only available spot at the front of the building, my old Honda CRV sandwiched between a white BMW and a blue Lamborghini.

"Wow! Where are we? A luxury sports car dealership?" I asked Holly. Stepping out, I took a close look at the two European cars, both shiny and spotless.

Holly said excitedly, "The Lamborghini belongs to the owner of the company. He drives to work and parks here on nice days. The white BMW is owned by a young entrepreneur of the company, who became a millionaire in his early 30s."

Entering the building, we walked up two flights of wide stairs to a security camera-supervised showroom. Its locking system was controlled from inside; outside there was a digital device on the metal frame at the entrance.

Holly pushed a button and gave her name through the speaker. The metal gate opened slowly. A friendly man with thick black hair and eyebrows, Italian according to Holly, courteously opened a glass door to the showroom. With a broad smile and in an absolutely charming manner, he greeted us, "*Nin hao!*" [您好！ How do you do?]

It was such a complimentary surprise, as I didn't expect anyone here to speak Chinese. I responded in Chinese, "*Nin hao*, too!" [您也好!]

"Thank you," the man answered politely.

From the other side of the showroom came the voice of a native Mandarin speaker. "Our company produces and sells limited edition luxury goods from European designers. We market them directly to consumers." I turned around toward the voice. A Chinese man in a blue print shirt was addressing a group of visitors. "We also offer fair business opportunity to every man and woman in the world. We would like to share the future growth of our company with you."

I gave Holly a suspicious look. Why had she brought me here? I had no interest in luxury goods. Along the wall, I saw hand-crafted leather shoes for men with toes pointed slightly upwards, and women's handbags made from animal fur, possibly zebra and leopard.

Inside a tall glass showcase in the far corner I saw two large handbags that appeared to be made from reptile skins. "Oh, Holly, look at those! Snake! Python, or maybe crocodile skin!" I suppressed an urge to scream. "Who in the world would want to carry cold-blooded reptilian skin on their shoulder?" I felt goose bumps on my back.

"You would be surprised, Pearl," said Holly with matter-of-fact calmness. "Hollywood stars seek custom-made, one-of-a-kind luxury goods to impress."

I stared at Holly, my colleague of twenty some years, surprising me today with a reference to Hollywood stars and their lifestyles. "Talking about Hollywood, did the Oscar nominations come out this year, Holly?" I was embarrassed by my ignorance, "I haven't seen any new movies for almost a year and I need to catch up. But who cares about the lifestyles of the movie stars?"

The Italian man came over and said, "Just last week we sold a python-skin handbag to a *da wan* [大腕, big wrist] from China."

"What did you just say?" Turning around, I gazed at him, amused. I was impressed. "May I ask your name, sir?"

"Aldo," he smiled, pointing at the embroidered nametag on his sleek designer black jacket uniform.

"You actually know the trendy Chinese word *da wan*?" I asked in disbelief. "Unbelievable, Aldo, really admirable!"

Aldo raised his right arm and twirled his hand a few times. With that gesture, I believed the man genuinely knew what he was talking about and also had a sense of humour. I returned the gesture. *Da wan* literarily means "big wrist," and refers to a very small group of Chinese who have powerful positions in Mainland China, such as CEOs of multinational Chinese corporations. *Da wan* could also refer to extremely wealthy Chinese, both men and women, with apparently unlimited purchasing power.

"Did the Chinese *da wan* ask for more exotic reptile skins?" I searched my mind for the name of a ridiculous reptile, "What about the skin of an Apatosaurus?"

Aldo burst out laughing. "I guess not yet, since that dinosaur has been extinct for millions of years."

Holly was signaling at me to move on. I knew she didn't want me to embarrass Aldo.

"*Yi hui er jian,*" [一會兒見! See you later] said Aldo in perfect Mandarin. I showed him two thumbs up.

Holly and I strolled down the showroom to a glamorous display of sparkling jewellery. The Chinese guy in the blue shirt came to us, having seen off the other group. "Are you enjoying the showroom, my friends?" he greeted us, and Holly introduced him to me as John, one of the luxury consultants in the company.

I noticed that John was wearing silver cufflinks and an oversized sports watch on his small wrist, from which reflected tiny precious stones.

John offered to guide us through the jewellery display. According to him, silver jewellery in the commercial market was usually 92.5 percent pure, but his company produced silver necklaces and rings from silver of 95 percent purity.

I noticed a large poster of the company's logo shimmering from behind a tall, double glass showcase. The poster showed a mother goose forcing its long neck and chubby body into the inner space of a goldfish tank. "Mother Goose," I murmured to myself, pointing at the poster for Holly to see. My friend looked puzzled before I realized I was thinking, out of context, about my friend Wendy, who was nicknamed Mother Goose.

After taking another look at the poster, I decided it could not possibly be a mother goose. It would have to be a romantic white swan. Designers have attached much more value, both aesthetic and monetary, to white swans.

Walking through the showroom with a professional guide was an eye-opening and ear-filling process. John told us that the owner of the company came from a European family that had produced handcrafted jewellery for two hundred years.

What: Share a Spring Dream

"Good morning! Opportunity knocks!" announced Holly, standing at my doorsteps on a foggy morning a week later. "The early bird catches the worm!" she remarked in a musical tone when I opened the front door to let her in.

I yawned and replied in a hoarse voice, "You know me, as a vegan, I don't care about worms for breakfast." She laughed. As we entered my eat-in kitchen, I asked her, "coffee or tea?"

She replied, "Guest follows the host, so whatever you like." She then wasted no time to announce some important business news. "Listen, Vegan Bird, in front of us there is a rare business opportunity for Chinese Canadians, especially in Toronto." Her eyes shone with excitement.

"Remember what we saw last week?" she asked earnestly.

"The ducklings, oh, they may actually be cygnets, baby swans! But not goslings." I answered as clearly as I could remember.

"What are you talking about? Ducklings or what? You didn't like my early-bird-catching-the-worm analogy, but now, you want to talk about waterfowls." It took me a minute to realize why she had burst out laughing again. I apologized for being out of context. I actually had the duckling and cygnet chat with Wendy, Mother Goose. Wendy and I sometimes shared an afternoon walk along the lake.

Holly attempted to get me back to the present. "Remember, just a few days ago, we visited the private showroom of World Wealth Waves Inc—WWW?"

Now I remembered the Italian man called Aldo who had greeted us in Mandarin. Holly was delighted. She said that WWW for the first time was opening its membership to the Chinese in Canada.

"Thank you for the information, but did they discriminate against Chinese money in the past?" I asked sarcastically.

"I don't think so; for business expansion, it's always timing and money." Holly continued, "Now WWW has its eye on the Mainland Chinese market, like many other companies in the world."

"Did you know this year the Chinese economy has started to decline? Millions of Chinese workers, including my nephew and your niece, may be laid off from offices and factories," I said.

"Indeed, their generation may face unemployment for the rest of their lives," lamented Holly. After a pause, she said hopefully, "The Chinese may have to embrace a new business model. This is the fifteenth year since China joined the WTO in 2000, so it must fulfil its obligation to open its domestic retail markets to the world."

Seated at the table, I poured steaming hot tea into two teacups to sooth our morning nerves. I also opened a box of almond cookies. Biting on the sweet cookie, I waited for my friend to tell me what I didn't already know.

Holly sighed and made a confession. "This may be the last opportunity for me to make some much-needed extra cash." Since her retirement a few years back, she said, she had to budget for every single thing. "What will happen when I am getting older? If we participate in the WWW business, perhaps I can make some extra income and save it for the future."

By the time we finished the morning tea, we had shared our financial problems and came up with an idea. Considering that WWW is a ten-year-old, established Canadian company, with its unique luxury products and a generous compensation system, we should seriously consider joining its sales team.

Why: Necessity Spring

I stood up from my computer desk, realizing it was time to go for a walk. A ten-minute drive to Ash Bridges Bay Park and a thirty-minute rapid walk by the lake would fulfil my New Year's resolution. I had managed to avoid cabin fever during the long Canadian winter by keeping this scheduled outdoor activity as a daily necessity. I also custom designed my route. Starting from the parking lot, I would take the whole loop of the Martin Goodman Trail, continue on the boardwalk, and return to the parking lot.

The winding Martin Goodman Trail goes around the edge of the lake, enclosing the bay for the yacht club. Two weeks before, I had seen some gulls standing frozen on the docks at the shallow water. These days, gulls were crying noisily and flying high above the lake. I looked for Mallard ducks and their ducklings, and swans with their cygnets, inside the bay; to my utter surprise, I found that the ducklings had already grown their full feathers, while the cygnets still looked more like ugly ducklings. The process of their maturity into beautiful swans would take three months. Now with their parents, the cygnets were also swimming on the edge of the open lake.

During my rapid loop, my mind was still preoccupied with Holly. Her distressing voice had made an imprint in my memory, which could not be easily erased or simply ignored. As a close friend and colleague of over twenty years, I thought I needed to do something. Regarding the WWW business, however, I imagined an interview for a luxury brand salesperson:

> Q: Can you name five luxury brand handbags in the market?
>
> A: LV, Coach, and—Gap, no not Gap . . .
>
> Q: Did you ever own a luxury handbag?
>
> A: I have a Gucci handbag.
>
> Q: Is it a certified product?
>
> A: I bought it from Xiu Shui in Beijing. The travel agent took us there.
>
> Q: I am sure it's a fake. Xiu Shui is notorious for marketing illegal imitations of European and American luxury brands.

Q: Do you wear high heels?

A: Never.

Q: Do you wear makeup?

A: Only lipstick.

Q: Sorry but you do not qualify for the job at this moment, although your honesty is appreciated. Once you have improved your knowledge of the luxury market, you are welcome to reapply for a starting position. Good luck.

I knew I didn't qualify, but if we joined WWW, we would expect the company to provide us with effective training. It dawned on me, however, that my decision should not be based on selling luxury products, but supporting my friend's business endeavour, because she needed to make extra income for her future.

Walking rapidly along the trail, I was inspired by the sight of the cygnets swimming with their parents on the edge of the open lake. If we joined WWW, we would need an incredible amount of support before we could understand this particular business. Would the WWW corporate leaders be responsible for guiding us to attain the success created by themselves?

I continued to walk up the hilly path, where many small birds lived in the thickets—sparrows, robins, wood pigeons, and others. I greeted them on sunny afternoons by clicking my tongue to create my version of a bird language. The birds usually turned their pretty feathered heads to look at me; after confirming that I was harmless, they quickly returned to seeking food. When that happened, I was quite convinced that we humans have some inter-species communication skills built into our genetic inheritance.

If we joined WWW, could we sustain our initial interest? When encountering indifference and rejection, would we be able to survive?

After completing the whole loop of the Martin Goodman Trail, I came to the boardwalk. At this spot, I often slowed down to ease my breathing. Standing on the real and artificial rocks here, I would face the lake in weather conditions, watching the white capped waves rushing in. They looked like a herd of white horses galloping towards the rocks before, with massive power, they crashed upon the rocks. With strong winter wind wailing in my ears, I had witnessed the most noisy, suicidal ending of the waves as they smashed onto the shore and shattered into millions of droplets of water.

According to Holly, this was the best time for us to join WWW. The Chinese government had announced that China would open its market. The CCTV, an official voice of the Chinese government, had confirmed that a golden era for internet-based direct sales would begin this year. How exciting if that were true! Only a year ago, such business was banned in China for leading people into dishonest pyramid schemes. And a decade ago, people were arrested for going to home-based business meetings, which were characterized as potential anti-government activities. What a world of changes!

It seemed that there had never been a better time for overseas Chinese to join WWW. Perhaps this new opportunity would allow ordinary people, such as retired teachers and other professionals, to participate in the world's fastest growing economy. We had been outsiders watching the Chinese Economic Reform when it started in the mid-1980s. The opportunity may have finally come for us.

Along the boardwalk there were a few tall poplars. I noticed a raccoon sitting on one of the bare branches, watching people and dogs going by under the tree. Walking along the sandy beach, I also noticed the lagoon change its size all the time, depending on the level of water in the lake; sometimes it would disappear entirely. Right now the lake was full after several spring showers, and the lagoon was quite a size. A large number of gulls and other birds were taking noisy baths. Occasionally, a dog waded in to chase the birds away, but soon they returned to continue their games.

There is an order of peace and balance in nature. I concluded that there was no need to worry too much about oneself, life is full of opportunities and new experiences. This might be a good time to join WWW, before the company entered the Chinese market. Most importantly, this would be my act of friendship for Holly.

Holly finally told me that, before she took me to the WWW showroom, she had already joined the company. I was relieved because her initial decision was not dependent on mine, it was her own. And persuading me to join WWW would be her next step toward expanding her business.

How: Sharing Spring Fever

Bright sunshine returned to Holly's face after I signed up to join her team. She sounded enthusiastic, with a specific goal to focus on. The subject of our conversations had changed to business development and product information instead of ducklings or Lake Ontario. I continued to share my walk with Wendy whenever we could.

Holly and I visited the WWW showroom more frequently. There was an urgent need for us to familiarize ourselves with existing luxury goods and new business opportunities. We started to memorize the introduction business script, which we had overheard many times when John was talking to visitors and potential new members. I realized that sooner or later we would be expected to deliver the same script to our own friends in order to expand the business.

"By the way, which Hollywood star wore WWW fashion jewellery? And at which year's Oscar Academy Awards?" I asked

John several times in the showroom. Finally, he said he had no idea, "The details are not important." He looked at me with some annoyance, as if I were harassing him. I tried to explain my intention, "There is an old saying in English, 'The devil is in the detail' and in case potential customers ask me, I hope I would be able to answer at least one of the two questions."

"Just tell them a *da wan* from China bought an exotic reptile skin handbag when you talk to your extremely rich Chinese friends," said John. Holly and I looked at each other, speechless. We knew that, in reality, we would have no chance to meet the famous celebrities from Hollywood, nor the extremely rich *da wan* from China. The rich and famous would use a direct VIP channel to meet with the CEO of the company.

I started to wonder what had attracted and persuaded Holly, and other ordinary Torontonians to join WWW. To become a diamond member, we had voluntarily opened our wallets and charged $5,000 on our credit cards, which was immediately converted to 8,000 WWW points for purchasing the company's luxury products, as well as participating in the potential business growth of the company. Did the glamorous items behind the glass display cases dazzle members' vision? Did the members think they would look as sexy and beautiful as the movie stars walking down the red carpet if they wore the same fashion jewellery?

At the end of that day, while driving towards Scarborough to drop off Holly, we had time to discuss why John hadn't bothered to answer our questions. Didn't he understand that the company's promotion should be solidly backed up with archives of factual dates and photos taken at the exact Oscar ceremonies?

Holly didn't have an answer, and after giving some serious consideration, she said she could only laugh at me for asking the same questions repeatedly. "Pearl, nobody would be as critical as you, when they heard marketing promotions anywhere."

In the end, I had to agree with Holly. Before we arrived at her apartment building, I asked her a totally different question, "By the way, do you remember who said, 'Vanity, vanity! Thy name is woman'?"

With a quick pause, Holly answered thoughtfully, "Sounds like a Biblical reference."

I disagreed, "It was probably Shakespeare," although I was not sure of the exact reference.

After several weeks, one Saturday morning at ten o'clock, Holly and I were sitting in a WWW training session. Looking around the classroom—surprise, surprise—there were more Chinese than the other races together. Were Chinese more risk-tolerant in business ventures? Or were Chinese more naïve than others to believe that quick money could be made in the market?

As the host of the training session, John, the luxury goods consultant, delivered an aggressive opening speech. "Remember, there is no free lunch. If you want to succeed, you need to double your efforts. Here is a simple formula, talk to twenty people daily and you may be able to quit your daytime job next year."

The full-day training session featured some success stories. A Chinese woman in her thirties, wearing a white lace dress with matching white high-heeled sandals, walked gingerly to the lectern at the front. I could tell she was wearing a pendent named *Three Times Triumphant*. Secret pride arose in me when I told Holly that I could instantly identify this emblematic piece of jewellery standing for the name of WWW.

"My name is Happy Woman!" announced the young woman and the audience burst out laughing. "I came to Canada last year with my husband."

Behind us, someone whispered, "Fresh off the boat." Holly nudged me with her elbow.

"Shortly after we landed, my husband went back to China to his former girlfriend—" the speaker suddenly broke down and started to weep over her misfortune.

Painful sounds of sympathy, long and short sighs, came from different corners of the room.

The rest of the story went like this: the abandoned, unhappy young woman met a WWW diamond member who introduced her to the company and her life had since changed dramatically. WWW became her new family in the new country. She had been involved in all of its business activities. Most recently, she had started to promote WWW to strangers. Within a month, she had successfully enrolled another new immigrant woman from her ESL class. She firmly believed she would be able to support herself in the future. "That's why I changed my name to Happy Woman!"

"Bravo! Happy Woman, what a story!" the audience hailed the courageous new immigrant.

Two other speakers also shared their personal experiences. One was a cleaning lady, who had promoted WWW products to her clients and now she had more than a dozen customers. The last speaker was a Black lady, who had a full-time job at one of the five major Canadian banks. She simply wore WWW rings and necklaces to work every day and within months many of her bank clients and colleagues had become her customers of WWW products.

At the end of the training session, John welcomed a young man called Renoir to give the crowd one more boost of energy. Renoir ran into the classroom energetically, like a star invited to a nightly talk show.

"*Da jia xia wu hao!*" [大家下午好! Good afternoon everyone!] Perhaps he didn't want to waste time on entertaining his audience and a single greeting served this purpose. "We need to hammer a few nails in at the end of the day." He asked, "How do you promote WWW products?"

Holly nudged me and I raised my hand, "By wearing WWW products."

Nodding, Renoir continued to quiz the class, "What is the effective way to promote WWW business?"

I nudged Holly this time. She raised her hand, "Talking to strangers about WWW business."

"Thank you! That's right! It's as simple as that!" The millionaire looked delighted that his simple recipes for success had been passed on to the new members. "Now I want to share with you what I have just learned from John today. Since many of you emigrated from Mainland China, I am pretty sure you all know this." Looking at his audience with expectation and curiosity, he asked them what was the most important instruction made by Deng Xiaoping in the mid-1980s that had jump-started the economic reform in China. Renoir waited for our response.

Holly was looking at me, I whispered, "Cross the river with your feet grabbing the pebbles?"

Meanwhile, Diana's voice rose above mine from the back, "White cat, black cat, so long as it catches a mouse, it is a good cat."

"That's it, the famous cat theory!" everybody agreed with Diana. "And what did Deng Xiaoping mean by that?" asked Renoir innocently.

"Oh, even kids in China know the answer, don't you?" The Chinese in the room were laughing when Diana spoke out again. "Deng Xiaoping meant the colour of the cat does not matter in economic reform, it is what the cat *does* that matters."

"But colour definitely matters in the business world in North America!" The Black woman stood up and stated. There was a small commotion among those in attendance.

Renoir paused for a few seconds and then he continued, "I believe Deng Xiaoping's 'white cat and black cat' theory can help us expand WWW business throughout the world."

Looking around the classroom, he said, "Now it's time to take action!" With his eyes shining, he said playfully, "Remember no discrimination against any cats. All cats are equally and warmly welcome to join the WWW business family. And I repeat WWW business door is open and inclusive to all cats: white cats, black cats, orange cats, long hair, short hair, pure breed, mixed breed, domestic, feral or wild cats, as well as the jealous cats in the musical *Cats*!"

Now we were all laughing with Renoir. Obviously, the group enjoyed being entertained rather than being lectured. Renoir concluded, "Now that you all know the secret recipes for success, nothing can stop you from achieving your goals. Good luck everyone!"

How: Spring into Action

Following the Saturday training session, Holly called me on Sunday afternoon. "Let's make a plan for the next two weeks, shall we? Do you think we can each find a potential recruit? How about taking them to the showroom on the second Wednesday afternoon? I will book John for a grand tour."

"Wow, taking action already!" I responded cheerfully. "Are you going to wear WWW products and talk to strangers?"

"Of course," said Holly seriously, "but I am not quite up to talking to strangers yet. Guess what, I actually wore my WWW big pearl fashion ring to church this morning. And I attracted a lot of attention from women of different age groups. A couple of young women liked it a lot. One actually tried it on her finger, but it wasn't her size, otherwise she might have asked me to sell it to her off my finger." Holly's voice expressed joyful new energy.

"That's so cool! Did you happen to wear your dangling pearl earrings to match?"

"No, maybe I should have, but I didn't want to look overdressed."

I totally understood her decision; we were, after all, modest and reserved former school teachers.

"By the way, Holly, I've also taken some action to add momentum to our team effort. While doing Tai Chi, I met a middle-aged Chinese woman in my neighbourhood. I think she might be interested in the WWW products or business."

"Well, that's great! We are definitely motivated! Let's invite these women to the showroom two weeks Wednesday afternoon!"

A journey of a thousand miles starts from beneath one's feet. Since I joined WWW with Holly, I had repeatedly heard this Chinese proverb in my head. It came from Lao Tzu, the only book the wise old man had ever penned in his life, *Tao Te Ching*, in 500 BCE.

Following the first steps beneath our feet, Holly and I had brought two guests, Ling and Waverly, to the WWW showroom on the second Wednesday afternoon. When we stepped through the secure entrance, Aldo, the Italian Canadian security guard, greeted our guests politely in Mandarin.

"*Nu shi men, nin men hao!*" [女士們,您們好! How do you do, Ladies!]

Both women stopped and looked alarmingly surprised. Then they started to giggle. Holly and I were delighted to see the dramatic effect of Aldo's Chinese greeting.

"*Qing wen xian sheng gui xing?*" [請問先生貴姓? May I ask Mister's respectful family name?] Waverly asked politely in the traditional Chinese manner.

"*Wo de xingming shi* Aldo Vitale, *qing jiao wo* Aldo." [我的姓名是 Aldo Vitale, 請叫我 Aldo. My full name is Aldo Vitale, please call me Aldo.]

Now our guests were excited beyond description. It was unbelievable that the Italian Canadian security guard not only could answer a question in Chinese, but also in traditional Chinese style. What a genius! Aldo shook everyone's hand, "*Huan ying, Huan ying!*" [歡迎，歡迎! Welcome, welcome!]

"Here comes the WWW Luxury Product Consultant," announced Holly. When John reached us, she formally introduced him to our guests. Following John, we started the twenty-minute grand tour, walking toward different display counters. I could tell that our guests were reluctant to start the tour as they wanted to have more fun with Aldo. Waverly kept turning back, as if looking for something.

After the tour, the usual procedure was to invite the guests to the training centre to talk about a business opportunity with WWW. However, both our guests expressed their interest in viewing WWW products. Ling wanted to see the diamond rings, because her son was shopping for an engagement ring for his fiancée. Waverly wanted to try on the French sunglasses.

Waverly and I walked around the corner of the L-shaped showroom toward the entrance area, where sunglasses, optics, and shoes were displayed. Aldo was dealing with a customer behind the counter. As soon as he saw us, he smiled. Waverly was delighted. With a shy smile, she asked me, "How much Chinese does Aldo speak?"

"I'm not sure," I answered honestly, before adding, "It looks to me he is serious about learning Mandarin."

"*Nu shi men* [女士們, Ladies], what can I do for you?" A smiling Aldo politely offered his service to us from behind the counter. I was waiting for Waverly to reply, but she suddenly became too self-conscious. She nudged me with her shoulder. I understood that she was expecting me to initiate the conversation. I introduced her to Aldo by her first name, and once Waverly overcame her shyness, she started to ask various questions about optical lenses and frames. Aldo addressed Waverly by her first name and I could see my guest was enjoying the courteous, respectful, verbal intimacy with Aldo. Most of the time, they were speaking English, but occasionally, Aldo used a few French words regarding the products manufactured in France. From time to time, Waverly inserted Mandarin into her conversation, when referring to Chinese cities, since many complex commercial products were made by multinational corporations in different Asian countries, especially in China.

While Waverly was still talking to Aldo, Holly and Ling came over to bid goodbye. Ling had driven that afternoon, so I was relieved from the responsibility of taking Holly home. It was only 4:30 pm in the afternoon, the sun was still high in the sky. Waverly was trying different pairs of sunglasses, and I was in no hurry to get home.

Around five o'clock, Aldo said he would finish work in half an hour and he would like to invite us to the Starbucks across the street. "I love Starbucks coffee!" Waverly responded immediately. Looking a bit embarrassed, she quickly covered her mouth with her hand. I smiled at them.

Half an hour later, the three of us were sitting in a cozy corner at the Starbucks. I asked Aldo casually, "How long have you been studying Chinese?"

Aldo tilted his head up, to recall. "About three years, ever since our company made a serious plan about entering the Chinese market."

"Did you take a course?" asked Waverly, curiously.

"I did, at the University of Toronto."

"No wonder your initial greeting was in a traditional Chinese style, polite and respectful," Waverly acknowledged, giving Aldo a big thumbs up.

"Thank you, Waverly," said Aldo, "Is that why you ladies were giggling at the entrance?"

"Honestly, we were very surprised, happily and unexpectedly,"

Waverly replied. "You made me use the same traditional style of greeting when I asked for your family name."

"Yes, you did, I noticed that," Aldo laughed heartily, "*Wo ke bu ke yi gei nin wo de dianhua haoma*?" [我可不可以給您我的電話號碼? May I give you my telephone number?]

Waverly looked a bit taken aback by Aldo's straightforward offer. She seemed quite happy to accept his contact information, though she looked a little puzzled. Aldo was quite different from the men she had known. She put Aldo's contact information inside her handbag happily.

"Good!" I clapped my hands, "A journey of a thousand miles starts from beneath one's feet. Do you know this ancient Chinese proverb, Aldo?"

"*Qian li zhi xing, shi yu zu xia.* [千里之行, 始於足下] My Chinese professor always uses this famous proverb to encourage us."

Later, while we were driving home, Waverly thanked me for inviting her to the WWW showroom. I congratulated her on the potential advance in her personal relationship. She said, "I never thought I would meet someone like Aldo. Pearl, I really hope he is my dream man."

"Don't forget, this is only the first step of a thousand-mile journey. It takes two people to fulfil the happiness in a joint life."

"Pearl, can you explain this to me? I was really puzzled when Aldo offered his phone number to me, why didn't he ask for mine? I would be willing to give it to him. Is this often the case with Caucasian men?"

"I don't think it was from a racial perspective, perhaps it is related to his culture or personality. A gentleman who respects a woman should, at least, leaves the decision to her for their first date."

"So, do you think Aldo is a gentleman?"

"That's a question for you to answer."

The following week, when Holly asked me to follow up with Waverly after the visit to the WWW showroom, I asked her about Ling's feedback. Ling said the diamond rings at WWW were priced much higher than in downtown Chinese jewellery stores or the jewellery stores in Hong Kong or New York City. Ling was not interested in fashion jewellery or other WWW products.

"So, there was no interest after all," Holly sounded disappointed.

"I didn't think it would be easy to attract customers in Canada or America," I told her my true opinion. "Your original idea was to expand the business in China."

"That is true, Pearl, China remains our best bet." She sounded hopeful again. "If Waverly could join our team it would help, since she is a recent immigrant from China. She would have many current connections in China."

I agreed.

How: Hopeful Spring vs Fruitless Summer

There was overwhelming anticipation that China would definitely open its domestic retail market to the world. WWW said the corporation had already opened its flagship store in Qing Dao to display its limited editions of European luxury goods. Gossip was flying high like a hot balloon about the immediate success of the flagship store and how Chinese customers had bought up all the displayed goods in the first week. WWW members with personal connections in Qing Dao had recruited over one hundred new members, each paying 15,000 yuan to become gold members. Many of them had their eyes set on the diamond rings and name-brand handbags.

Holly and I decided to review our potential human resources in mainland China. On a sunny afternoon after an energetic walk, we sat on a park bench facing Lake Ontario. Holly had brought a

map of China. Starting from Shanghai, where we both had friends
and relatives, the colour marker in her hand moved slowly across
the map from east to west, from Shanghai to Chong Qing, the
biggest inland city in Western China. Along that line, she placed
some dots. Then she repositioned her marker to Harbin in northern China and drew a line heading south, passing Beijing, Tianjin,
Zhengzhou, Wuhan, Zhuzhou, Guangzhou and all the way to
Hainan Island across the South China Sea. Along this line, she
placed many more dots.

It was truly amazing that, between us, we shared more than one
hundred relatives, friends, and old classmates. Most of them were
retired professionals, now full-time grandparents raising their
grandchildren at home. If we could persuade a quarter of them to
join WWW, we would have quite a number of associates to bring
the WWW logo to different parts of China. Leaning back against
the park bench, Holly looked at the white sails far out on the lake.
After a long moment of silence, with her eyes half closed, she let
out a sigh of relief as she visualized a bright future.

"WWW could bring profit to us through unlimited generations," she mumbled, as if talking to herself. "I am not dreaming of
becoming a millionaire, but if I could earn an extra $3,000 income
per month, I would also call myself Happy Woman!"

The tranquility of the park filled me with inner peace, as Lake
Ontario shimmered under the sunny sky, reflecting its transparent
blue colour. At this particular moment, I would not trade my spot
for anywhere else in the world. The Chinese retail market seemed
too remote to be of any relevance.

A flock of Canada geese called, flying over the lake in a large for-
mation, returning home from their winter migration. "Wonderful
birds," uttered Holly, "they always remember their homeland."

While the geese were calling with loud cries from the blue
sky, I was suddenly reminded of a Chinese fable that my mother

used to tell. Once upon a time, two brothers were out hunting, and when they saw a flock of geese flying overhead, they started arguing fiercely about how to cook a goose for dinner. Before they finally agreed on a particular recipe, the geese had flown far away, beyond the range of their bows and arrows. I was alarmed by the coincidental similarity between this fable and our current situation with WWW and China.

For the rest of the afternoon, I was haunted by the image of the geese.

While we were waiting anxiously for the CEO of the company to update us on the Chinese market, the CBC morning news reported that the cherry blossoms in Toronto's High Park were having their most sensational season this year. Tens of thousands of Torontonians, plus more thousands from the satellite cities in the Greater Toronto Area, were thronging to High Park every day. My Tai Chi and meditation friends had organized a ritual Japanese Sakura Hanami to rejuvenate our spiritual and physical energy. They chose a Thursday morning in order to avoid the large crowds. It could be the last opportunity before the white and pink cherry blossoms snowed down in the wind, and I decided to invite Waverly.

April is a delicate spring month in Toronto, sometimes sunny, sometimes cloudy, other times rainy, or even snowy. Thursday morning was bright and sunny. As soon as I stepped out of the subway station I saw Waverly standing at the entrance of High Park, a tall slim woman among others. I waved at her and she waved back. I could see that she was wearing the French designer sunglasses from WWW and they looked perfect on her with her straight black hair reaching below her shoulders.

"You look outstanding, Waverly! The sunglasses really suit you," I said as she came forward to give me a hug. I noticed that she was also wearing a WWW necklace, called Spring Rain Drops, with matching earrings.

"Are you modelling for WWW products?" I joked.

"How did you know?" she asked.

"I was only joking. Tell me, did the company hire you to model?"

She nodded. "Only occasionally. Thanks to Aldo's strong recommendation. Once WWW officially enters the Chinese retail market, I will be working full-time. Aldo and I will be sent to China to help set up showrooms in different cities, and to train local staff and members."

"Wow, congratulations! How incredible! Your career and personal life are progressing together!"

"I want to thank you, Pearl, for inviting me to the WWW showroom initially. You are our *hong niang* [紅娘, match-maker], I want to take you out for lunch today, do you have time after Hanami?"

"Of course, I do, Waverly, I am truly happy for you and Aldo!"

The day after our Hanami, it was reported that the cherry blossoms had drifted down in the overnight rain. Right after the morning news, Waverly called to thank me again for bringing her to the cherry blossom ritual. She said she felt a deep joy for being in tune with nature's rhythms.

The rest of that spring swept across the land with its warm breeze. Delicate lemon green burst out on waving willow branches by the lakeshore, while bright yellow dandelions were blooming everywhere. Within a week, small leaves were budding out on trees across the city. Birds were calling their mates on high branches. Within another week, caterpillar- and propeller-shaped seeds were flying in the air. In a short time, thick summer foliage had covered the trees. Then breezes felt sweaty and the hot sun tanned the skin red. Most Torontonians wore summer T-shirts and shorts. Young women wore sleeveless tank tops matched with floral short skirts or lacy white jean shorts.

In midsummer, WWW excitedly launched its high heels and flats and new fashion jewellery with Asian motifs. Holly and I were among the audience who clapped for our friend Waverly walking proudly down the showroom's catwalk, launching the new products. Unfortunately, the jewellery was not to my taste. I was still too shy to wear a string of chunky, colourful fashion jewellery to attract attention on the street. Holly and I both shied away from the pretty new flat heels priced at $900 a pair. In fact, we were both waiting for orthopedic surgery appointments to correct our overgrown big toes.

Recently WWW Chinese group leaders had started daily communication with the members via WeChat, a smartphone app from China. Without going to the training centre, we were receiving meeting schedules, holiday greetings, and a daily moral boost. Many of the messages consisted of cartoon emojis called "red rose," "shining sun," "thumbs-up," "clapping hands," and even "a canon shooting out 'welcome' to new members." It seemed to us that our group leaders were preparing the members to be air-dropped soon into Mainland Chinese retail markets.

That summer progressed from burning heat during the day to sweaty humidity throughout the night to eventually hit the hottest day recorded on earth since 1881 according to NASA. Cottage owners fled the city. Others stayed inside their air-conditioned homes or spent their days in shopping malls, public libraries, and cinemas, or soaking in the outdoor public swimming pools. It was understandable that there were fewer WWW activities during those languid, hot summer days. But why had the group leaders discontinued emoji stickers to the members?

When the long exhausting summer finally started to wane, we had growing doubts about whether WWW would ever officially enter the Chinese market. There were rumours and stories about the Chinese bureaucracy and large hidden costs. And it turned out that WWW did not get a license to legalize its business in China. The company finally realized that it had never possessed the resources to compete in the wild jungles of the Chinese market.

Why: WWW Not a Winner

At the end of the summer, when sugar maples in my neighbourhood shot their radiant red colour into the sky, Wendy returned from her annual summer trip to her hometown in Yorkshire, England.

"Welcome home, Mother Goose! How was your trip this year?" I asked.

"There are so many Chinese tourists in Europe," reported Wendy, "busload after busload. I tried to talk with a few to find out where in China they had come from. Unfortunately, they don't speak English."

"Did you see them in Yorkshire?" I asked. I knew that Yorkshire was the base of the industrial revolution. "Did the Chinese come to visit the cotton mill powered by the huge waterwheel?"

"You mean the water-driven looms from the 1770s? Do you actually think the Chinese would be interested in seeing the old mill buildings?"

"Maybe not. They probably wanted to visit London for the Queen's ninetieth birthday celebrations. They must have visited Buckingham Palace."

"Some international tourists were there, but not too many Chinese, they apparently went somewhere else."

"Then it must be the British Museum or Windsor Castle or Stonehenge in Salisbury?"

"Oxfordshire," Wendy said slowly, allowing me to catch up with the geography of England.

"Oxfordshire? Oh, where Oxford is? The Chinese believe

education is the only pathway to wealth and equality in the world."

"I am not so sure about that," remarked Wendy doubtfully.

"How so?"

"You may want to Google a new iconic hot spot, Bicester Village in Oxfordshire. It is the current focus of Chinese tourists. It could potentially be the most valuable business information for lucrative retail business," Wendy laughed cynically. "So how is your summer? Are you keeping up with your New Year's resolution?"

"What resolution?" My mind went blurry. What had I promised to do?

"Do you have time? Let's go for a walk by the lake tomorrow afternoon, shall we?"

Wendy changed the topic, reminding me of what I used to do every afternoon in early spring.

"Sure, I'll call Holly to see if we can all go for a nice walk together."

It was a beautiful autumn day with blue sky and a few brilliant white clouds. Wendy, Holly, and I met at the Martin Goodman Trail near Ash Bridges Bay. Both my friends had been walkathon activists. Before we set off, they reset their step-calculators to zero. According to Wendy, post-menopausal women should walk 7,000 steps daily to effectively prevent osteoporosis and bone density loss.

"I found it easier to do when I was travelling," said Wendy.

After some basic warm-up exercises, we set off with long strides toward the rising slope of the trail, then down to the wooden dock of the Yacht Club. This time of year, boats were in and out making the small bay look like a busy port. However, instead of bringing back their catch of the day to sell on the dock, as in other parts of the world, the owners of the pleasure boats rushed into the Club House to buy BBQ hot dogs, hamburgers, and cold beer. There were no Mallard ducks or lake gulls within the bay at this time of the year; the birds were looking for fresh fish out in the lake instead of waiting to scavenge food from the humans.

"Have the cygnets, or ugly ducklings all grown up?" Wendy asked me, smiling.

"Absolutely, Mother Goose, they have all transformed into beautiful swans!"

We continued along the trail around the tip of the peninsula. "Wasn't this place a landfill originally?" I asked Wendy since she had lived in the neighbourhood for more than four decades.

"Oh, yes, it was a disgusting, smelly landfill for many years."

"Hard to believe," Holly commented, "how long did it take for nature to do the makeover? Look at the tall trees now, amazing . . . "

By the time we reached the end of the trail at the boardwalk, our lungs were filled with fresh oxygen and our leg muscles felt tightened. Sitting down on a bench at the top of a slope, we felt a cool lake breeze caress our foreheads. I closed my eyes.

"Are you dozing off?" Holly nudged me with her elbow. I rose quickly from the bench to stretch my legs and swing my arms. "What are we going to do about the WWW business?" I asked.

"What business?" Wendy asked curiously. "Did you start a business while I was away?"

"Yes. To make white cats and black cats into entrepreneurs."

"Marketing limited-edition luxury goods," answered Holly properly.

"By the way, Pearl, did you Google Bicester Village in Oxfordshire?" Wendy asked me.

"Sorry, I forgot all about it," I apologized.

"You and I were discussing where Chinese tourists chose to visit in England," Wendy reminded me. "Now let me tell you where most of them went. They went to Bicester Village in Oxfordshire, a famous luxury shopping outlet for high-end boutiques."

"Why?" I asked a stupid question.

"To buy famous brands like Prada, Gucci, DKNY, Burberry and so on at discount prices."

"Do you know the price range of those name brands?" Holly asked earnestly.

"I'm not sure . . . a thousand British pounds for a handbag, I heard."

"That's ridiculous!" Holly exclaimed.

"Are you all right?" Wendy touched Holly's arm.

"Oh, I'm okay, but let me tell you something—" Holly was speechless for a few long seconds. It was obvious that something had seriously upset her.

Finally, she had recovered. "Two months ago, I ordered a WWW luxury handbag," she said, "a birthday present for my niece in Shanghai. You won't believe what the young woman said after receiving my present."

"She thanked her dear aunt in Canada for sending her a luxury birthday present," I said.

"No, no, no, not a single word of gratitude! When I called on her birthday, she was actually angry at me. She said, 'Aunty, please don't be upset, I have given the bag to my mother, because it didn't suit me. My mother said you've lived in Canada for too long, you are not in touch with young people in China. We only want to carry name-brand handbags.'" Taking a deep breath, Holly continued, "I told her, 'You will hear about the WWW brand soon. At that time, you may even want to become a luxury product consultant. It will be a great opportunity for you to earn extra income, if you can sell WWW products to your friends.'"

"What did your niece say?"

"She said . . . listen to this," Holly turned to Wendy, "what was the brand-name handbag you just mentioned, P—something?"

"Oh, you mean Prada?"

"Yes, Prada. My niece said her friend's aunt bought her niece a Prada handbag on Boxing Day last year. It only cost $3,000 Canadian dollars for a true signature luxury handbag!"

I wanted to ask Holly why she had never mentioned her conversation with her niece to me before or after I joined WWW. But I decided to let it go, it was no longer important. How could an old retiree living on a limited pension in Toronto possibly satisfy her niece's vanity dream in Shanghai?

My pipe dream that I had secretly cherished suddenly collapsed in front of my eyes like sand on the beach. How could I ever have believed that I could help my friend build up her pension reserves? Or to offer a solution to my nephews and nieces in China if they were unemployed? I felt myself slipping into an abyss of despair, which wasn't simply because of my own naïvete and ignorance, but the sudden revelation that the world was driven by an insatiable desire to possess one or more famous brand handbags. This contagious disease had already spread like a pandemic among the younger generation in China. Holly's niece had the outrageous fortitude to tell her aunt that a $3,000 Prada handbag would save her from becoming a laughingstock among her peers. In reality, Holly's birthday gift for her niece wasn't cheap at all, but it was not among the famous brand handbags established as a symbol of elite or wealth. And so Holly's birthday gift was received as an insult by the girl.

Holly and I stopped talking about WWW business or the Chinese retail market.

Why: Good News vs Bad News

Starting sometime in mid-September, my neighbourhood streets became dramatically colourful. It was the fall season. I felt an emotional impulse to go out and walk around the blocks almost every day after dinner. One night, with a full moon in the sky, I was guided somewhat by the image of a traditional Chinese ink painting. Filled with romantic sentiments, I decided to walk across Monarch Park towards India Town. Under the mysterious silver moonlight, I saw Waverly and Aldo sitting on a park bench for two, cuddling in each other's arms. My heart beating fast, holding my breath, I quietly passed behind their backs without being noticed. Once out of their peripheral vision, I stopped to appreciate the perfect picture of two lovers in their private time and space under the moonlight.

A few days later Waverly called to invite me to lunch at a downtown Italian restaurant. "I have something important to share with you."

"That's great! I am looking forward to hearing it," I answered delightedly.

After hanging up, I asked myself what could be the important thing that Waverly wanted to tell me. Most likely, she and Aldo had gotten engaged. That must be it! Looming in front of my eyes was the perfect picture of the lovers cuddling in the moonlight.

It was a beautiful day to go out with my pretty girlfriend. Waverly and I took the subway to St Andrew Station and walked from there until we spotted a shady tree, and we ran and sat down on the grass.

"I've good news and bad news, what do you want to hear first?" Waverly gazed at me through her French sunglasses. She waited until I made my choice.

"Good news, please."

"OK, the good news is big!" Waverly was excited, "Aldo and I are engaged!" She stretched out her right hand. The blue sapphire ring was sparkling in the sun.

"Wow! I have guessed it right! Congratulations, Waverly!"

"A few days ago, on a bright full moon evening, he said to me, 'Let's go to the park, it will be much more romantic.' So, we went, the moon was so bright that night. After I sat down on the park bench, Aldo got down on his knee and asked me to marry him. Some people gathered around us, urging me to say yes. It was an incredible moment, so I said 'Yes.' The passersby were clapping as if they were special guests invited to attend the ceremony. Aldo gave me a long kiss and put the ring on my finger."

"Guess what, Waverly, that night, I passed behind the park bench where you and Aldo were sitting." I burst out with my side of the story. "It must have been after your engagement because there was no crowd then."

"Really? Why didn't you talk to us?"

"I didn't want to disturb the lovers. You were cuddling in each other's arms." I laughed.

"That's true, so in a sense, you did witness my engagement. Had I known Aldo's plan, I would have invited you. You are like a sister to me in Canada." Waverly stretched out her long arms to pull me closer to her for a hug.

It was time for lunch. I didn't really want to know what possibly could be the bad news from Waverly. We got up from the grass and went down a pathway to a large underground commercial area. There, past a lot of retail stores, Waverly led me directly to an Italian restaurant, where we each ordered a lunch of three delicious courses: a fresh garden salad, an appetizer of sautéed mushrooms or zucchini, and finally a main course of angel-hair pasta, topped with garlic shrimps in home-made tomato sauce. When we had a cup of black coffee to complete our lunch, I didn't know what else could make me more contented.

As I was seriously thinking about where to spend the rest of the afternoon, Waverly stared at me and reminded me, "You haven't asked me about the bad news yet, was that intentional? If you really don't want to know, I don't blame you."

"Oh, Waverly, the good lunch has given us energy to handle the bad news. What is it?"

"Let's go then," said Waverly, standing up from the table.

"Why? Please sit down and share the news with me."

"Let's go. I need to show you something." Waverly picked up my jacket from the coat stand. I was too astounded to see that Waverly had something serious on her mind. We headed back toward the staircase leading to street level.

Next to the staircase was a women's fashion store, where samples of jackets, sweaters, skirts, and other garments were hanging on metal racks outside the store entrance. Waverly stopped and whispered to me, "If you see anything familiar inside the store, don't be alarmed. Just keep looking for familiar items. We will ask about prices and manufacturers." I nodded in total confusion.

The owner of the store was a petite Chinese lady, probably from Guangzhou or Hong Kong; she greeted us in Cantonese. I followed Waverly closely as we moved carefully around the clothed mannequins in order to get to the far end. Built into the corner were glass shelves used to display fashion jewellery sitting inside open boxes. I was surprised to see a few familiar items from the WWW catalogue, displayed here in different packaging boxes. Then I saw something similar to what I had recently purchased: a silver necklace with two tear-drop shaped dangling pendants of artificial sparkling crystals.

Without further hesitation, I picked the set up. While I was examining it, the owner of the store came by. "That is a pretty necklace for either dressing up or daily wearing," she said, "it's also one of the few high-purity silver items in the market."

"What do you mean by high purity silver?" I asked curiously. Waverly nodded at me for asking the right question.

"Most of the silver jewellery in the market is of 92.5 percent purity, but this company has produced silver jewellery of 95 percent purity," the woman replied, reminding me of what I had heard many times when John, the WWW luxury goods consultant, was talking to visitors during their grand tour. Now that I had heard the same thing from a tiny independent store owner in an underground concourse downtown, alarm bells were ringing in my ears.

"Do you know the name of the company that produced it?" My heart was beating fast in my chest. I was expecting the owner to say "WWW." Instead, she went back to her counter and returned a few minutes later; she showed us a receipt printed in simplified Chinese characters saying Yi Wu Gold and Silver Jewellery Inc. I examined the small jewellery box and noticed printed at the bottom the words, Made in China.

"Do you want to try it on?" asked the woman. "Here is a mirror."

Holding my breath tightly, I asked her softly, "How much is the necklace?"

Waverly nodded at me from behind the store owner.

"Thirty dollars. If you pay cash, I won't charge you the taxes."

I was stunned. It was sold at $150 plus taxes by WWW. I didn't utter a sound, continued to hold myself steady, as if considering her offer.

"Try it on. You'll see how pretty it is!"

Meanwhile, Waverly picked up two fashion rings, "How much for the rings?"

She tried on the big pearl ring that Holly had bought from WWW for $120 plus taxes.

"Twenty-five dollars for the big ring, again if you pay cash, I won't charge you taxes."

"Is it also made by Yi Wu Gold and Silver manufacturer?" Waverly asked.

"All the nicer silver jewellery came from the same company. I was in Yi Wu during the Chinese New Year, and I ordered these new products because of their style and quality."

"How is your business doing here?" Waverly changed the topic.

"Not good," the owner exhaled a soft sigh. "You see, most people who come down here for lunch work in the offices upstairs or in the nearby buildings. Few tourists or pedestrians would walk down here from the street. Thank you for dropping by my store."

"I would like to buy the big pearl ring," I said cheerfully. "Do you have size seven-and-a-half?"

"There is no half size for fashion rings, get size eight. With a large ring like this, you will need more room to put it on or take it off your finger." The owner knew more about the products than John of WWW. As I met Waverly's eye, I asked her, "Would you like one, Waverly? My gift for you."

Waverly nodded her head toward the exit, indicating we should leave. I paid the owner twenty-five dollars cash, and she placed the jewellery box inside a pretty shopping bag for me.

Back at street level, we walked into the remaining Indian-summer weather where the slanting shadows of the skyscrapers had shaded the sidewalks along the entire street. "It is too early to go home," said Waverly, pulling me into a roadside coffee shop where we found a nice rooftop table for ourselves.

"What do you think of my shades, Pearl?" Waverly touched her French sunglasses.

"You look super cool," I said admiringly. "Are you sure they were not made in Yi Wu?" I teased her.

"Not a doubt. They were made in France. The shades were a gift from Aldo, I have the original case at home."

"Yi Wu probably made both the sunglasses and the cases," I continued to tease her logically. "All the products I have bought from WWW had expensive boxes embossed with a silver swan. None of the boxes were printed 'Made in Italy' or 'Made in France', of course, it didn't have 'Made in China' either."

"I can't believe we were cheated by the Canadian company that's been around for two hundred years! We should sue WWW for its dishonesty. Its premeditated scheme to deceive the members is backed by solid evidence."

"By the way, how did you find out about this, did Aldo know?" I asked.

"Of course, he did." Pulling her sunglasses off her face, she said in a whisper, "Three weeks ago, after we had accidentally discovered the truth, he resigned from the company. They closed down the showroom last week for good. The company said it had lost all its investment in the China endeavour."

"Is this the bad news?" I asked Waverly. She nodded, putting the sunglasses back on her face. We went back to sipping the cold drinks in our tall glasses.

Epilogue: Who We Are

Around mid-October, colourful foliage in our neighbourhood had gradually reached the peak of the season; shortly after, almost simultaneously, all leaves turned into one rusty colour. Before Halloween, piles of dry fallen leaves had curled up on the sidewalk where they would run with the wind like departing ghosts of the current season. Holly, Wendy, and I continued to meet for walks throughout the autumn.

By November, except for the evergreens, all other trees had lost their leaves along our walking path. Their bare branches, reaching out toward the sky in sunshine or moonlight, appeared naked and stark. One early December afternoon when we reached the boardwalk as usual, we climbed up the big rocks to watch the waves on Lake Ontario. A few large flocks of Canada geese were flying close to the lake surface in energy-saving formations, departing on their annual journey to the distant, sunny destinations.

I raised my voice to its peak toward the sky, "Bon voyage, Waverly and Aldo!" I started waving my arms in big circles at the geese, "Bon voyage, Waverly and Aldo!"

Wendy and Holly turned their heads to me with alarmed expressions. Holly shouted at me from the top of another piece of big rock, "What happened to Waverly and Aldo?"

Wendy also raised her voice high, "Did they go back to China?"

When we all came down to the ground, I told them softly, "They left for Taiwan this afternoon."

"For their honeymoon? Or for holidays?" Wendy asked.

"Aldo will be going to the National Taiwan University to attend graduate school for his MA in Chinese. Waverly has a couple of job interviews in the next two weeks. She wants to work in a bilingual, bicultural tech company in Taiwan for a few years."

Christmas was approaching. This year, strangely enough, my girlfriends and I were looking forward to Boxing Day shopping like teenagers. We had our eyes set on a certain wearable, technical athletic device for some time, but unlike impatient teenagers, we were willing to wait for a better deal.

On December 27, the three of us took the subway downtown to the old Eaton Centre to get our new toy. We knew exactly what we wanted, the brand and the price. After spending an hour in the crowded store, pushing in and out among parents and their tech-savvy kids, we were served by the store staff. Considering the availability of all the fitness trackers and their prices, we decided to stick to our original choice of a decent, medium-priced fitness tracker with reliable functionality. Eventually, following our individual tastes, Holly chose one with an orange wristband, Wendy a creamy white, and I love purple.

In the afternoon of New Year's Eve, we met for our vigorous daily walk as usual. When we reached the junction of Martin Goodman Trail and the boardwalk, we stopped on the artificial slope, surrounded by dark green holly bushes with bright red berries. For our New Year's resolutions, we promised each other that we would reach 8,000 steps daily in the coming spring, before the Canada geese returned home. We held up our wrists toward the sky, our new athletic watches reflecting the sunshine, the wristbands like three colourful leaves left on bare branches.

Leftover Women

Opal

Stepping off the escalator above the subway, I entered the dentist's office. My glance fell on a fresh green bouquet sitting on the high counter, its white and light green blossoms arranged tastefully in a matching vase; instantly, I felt a soothing relief from the summer heat outside. In the corner of the room, on top of the coffee table, a pile of current magazines awaited readers. I sat down on the edge of the couch, and leaned forward to select my casual reading. My eyes latched onto a new name, *Zoomer* magazine, with a photo of Margaret Trudeau in a red dress on the cover.

Before I had a chance to read the featured story, I found myself sitting in the reclining dentist chair with a pair of oversize dark goggles covering my eyes. My hygienist, Opal, of South Asian descent and in her late thirties, stood beside me with an array of sterile dental tools. Opal has been my hygienist for over a decade. I used to have my teeth cleaned three times a year when I had a deluxe dental insurance plan. Upon retirement, I have reduced my dental appointments to once a year. In the past decade, during my frequent visits, Opal and I developed an on-going conversation about personal matters, hers and mine. While her hands were busy scraping coffee and tea stains from my teeth, she acted as the primary speaker between us. From time to time, when she needed my participation, she would ask a simple, yes-no question, which required only a nod of my head or shake of my hand. If an answer invited elaboration, I only wished I had two mouths, one for her to work on, the other to answer her questions.

Now reclining comfortably in the dentist chair, I wait for Opal to start our conversation. Although she sometimes talks about the weather with me, the topic she brings out today surprises me. She discloses a woman's top secret without hesitation—she will be forty-eight years old in August. I mumble my disbelief, "No way!"

"Yes, I am," confirms Opal seriously, "and I'm still single, waiting to meet a man seriously interested in marriage."

I want to ask her whether she thinks it's all right to be single at forty-eight. While Opal suctions the saliva from my mouth, she continues in a self-mocking tone, "I am a typical 'leftover woman' as you Chinese would say these days."

"What?" This time I pull the dark goggles off my face. I gaze at her with a startled expression, "Leftover what?"

"Woman."

"Like leftover food? Do you actually feel that way?" I stare at her, demanding an answer. "Where did you pick up this derogatory phrase?"

Opal chuckles, "From my Chinese clients, of course." Adjusting the goggles over my face, she continues to clean my teeth. Our conversation is temporarily suspended until she is ready to resume. It takes her a few long minutes to search through the entangled gossip she has overheard from her clients. According to her, "leftover woman" is an accepted Chinese term coined by a national women's organization in China. It refers to a single woman in China, between 27 and 44 years of age, who has never been married. Opal says that several Chinese clients have told her that the term is widely used in the Chinese official media, including TV, radio, and newspapers. She raises her eyebrows, "One Chinese client said the term has even been included in the Chinese national census." She is surprised that I have never heard about this hot phrase before.

Opal asks me to lift my chin, so she can clean my upper teeth. I take the chance to ask her a personal question, relevant to our conversation, "Tell me, did you ever want to be married?"

"Mm, yes, or—maybe no," Opal answers with obvious vacillation. "It all depends on whom I would be married to." I agree with her, nod my head.

With my head tilting back, I can see Opal's face from beneath her eye level. Her large brown eyes are outlined by thick black eyelashes, the lashes curl outward naturally without any sticky cosmetic mascara. When she blinks and focuses, her eyes disclose the inner mysteries of her emotions, like windows partially open or closed. I have no doubt that Opal's beautiful eyes are the envy of her female clients, including me for sure. I am also aware of her long-legged, slim athletic figure. I would be willing to work extremely hard to sculpt my body into something like hers. Now that my memory is activated, I remember Opal has been a runner for the annual Terry Fox Run and other causes in our city. I also recall that she was supposed to take a trip back to Pakistan to visit her old father last year. When Opal reaches back for another dental tool, I take the opportunity to rush my question in. "How is your Dad?"

"Who? Oh, my father? Thank you for remembering him." Opal seems surprised, but she answers flatly without emotion. "I did make it back to Karachi last summer before he passed away. Shall I tell you about my trip?" Her beautiful eyes are inquiring. I nod my head several times with the shady goggles on my face.

To make Opal's long story short, her parents were both high school teachers in Karachi. In the 1970s, she says, Karachi was a prosperous metropolis in South Asia like New York in North America today. From the late 1980s to 1990s, ethnic riots and political violence broke out in their city. The Pakistani government deployed troops to restore order. Belonging to an endangered minority in Pakistan, Opal's parents came to Canada as refugees with their two daughters. After settling down in the Scarborough area, her parents eventually managed a small South Asian grocery store for a living. Her sister married a Hindu and has three children. After spending ten years in Canada, her father decided to return to Karachi to resume his teaching career before reaching retirement age. Opal and her mother continue to live in their bungalow in Scarborough today.

"Do you know why I needed to visit my father before his death?" Opal asks me.

I want to say because he was your dad. I also want to ask her whether her culture requires adult children to perform filial duties and funeral rituals at a parent's death. But I can't start a discussion with a dental tool still inside my mouth, so I wave my left hand. Opal has to answer her own question. After another pause, she says slowly, "I needed to know my father's last wish for me, especially if it was different from his previous intent."

"What did you find out?" I ask.

"My father made it ever so clearer to me as he had firmly stated in the past in Canada. He told me again that regarding my marriage, I should never marry a Karachiite-type, Urdu-speaking Pakistani man. He said that he and my mother sacrificed their careers and happiness by coming to Canada as refugees, so that their two daughters would not marry Pakistani men."

"Ouch," I scream. Instantly, Opal stops flossing my teeth.

"Are you OK?" she asks anxiously, her beautiful eyes frowning.

I tell her I just want to say that I am very sorry to hear that her father disliked his countrymen with such a categorical rejection. I don't know how to comment on her father's racial and religious bias.

"But Opal," I push her hands away, "you live in Canada, shouldn't your marriage be your own decision? Did you happen to love a man forbidden by your father?" I ask suspiciously.

"Of course, I did, a handsome Urdu-speaking young man from Pakistan. Because my father refused to approve our relationship, we continued to delay our marriage year after year until now, when I have become a Leftover Woman." Opal spits out her last sentence with a sneer. I am deeply troubled by Opal's despondence. Years after her father had returned to Pakistan, Opal says she was hoping that he would change his mind. Now that her father has passed away, will Opal be obligated to live under the spell of the last verdict held by the dead man?

We do not have enough time to discuss Opal's future plans before she has finished cleaning my teeth. She places my chart on the high counter in the waiting room for the receptionist. Before calling her next patient, she says, "Why don't we meet for coffee some time? Make it before your next dental appointment."

"Great idea," I smile at Opal with my freshly cleaned teeth, reluctantly swallowing our unfinished conversation. I have made a mental note that our next meeting should be sooner than next summer.

Jade

Standing on the moving escalator, I descended to the subway platform. Within a few minutes, a southbound train stopped in front of me. I quickly stepped into a car. In front of my eyes stood my next-door neighbour, Jade Yang! What was the probability of two neighbours to meet on a subway train? What a surprise!

Jade's family moved into our neighbourhood about a decade ago. She is a registered nurse, her husband, Tie Sheng, a mechanical engineer, and their daughter, Silver, a science student attending university. The couple works on night shifts all year round except some weekends. We rarely bump into each other on our street, not even on our shared landing for the back entrances of our attached townhouses.

Now sitting down in a cozy seat for two, letting out a deep breath, we start to appreciate a rare intimacy for the first time. Shortly after the train pulls out noisily from the station, Jade tugs my sleeve and whispers into my ear, "Pearl, did you hear any noise from my house last Sunday night?"

"Last—Sunday—night?" I repeat slowly, unwinding my memory. "Was I home?"

"Yes, you were," she confirms softly, "your kitchen lights were on."

But I can't recall anything in the neighbourhood that has left any traces in my memory. Jade starts to offer some details. "Around nine thirty last Sunday night, we had finished dinner but were still sitting around the table. My husband and my daughter had a dispute, he was yelling and shouting. He ordered Silver to stop seeing her boyfriend. Otherwise, he threatened to break her legs."

"My goodness, what's wrong with him?" I burst out in disbelief.

Jade continued, "Silver stood up from the table and shouted back at her father. Crying loudly, she ran upstairs and shut the door. Around midnight, she came down with a suitcase, slamming her bedroom door angrily behind her. She swore not to come back home unless her father stopped interfering with her life. She left with her boyfriend, who came to pick her up."

I can't believe that behind the common wall we have shared for a decade, there has been ancient warfare between a controlling father and a rebellious daughter regarding her future marriage. "What makes your husband so adamantly dislike his daughter's boyfriend?" I ask Jade.

"The young man is *Han*," Jade says seriously.

"Do you mean Chinese?" I respond suspiciously.

Jade confirms, "Yes, the boyfriend is *Han*, Chinese."

"What's the problem then? What's wrong with a Chinese girl dating a Chinese boyfriend?" I am truly puzzled. I hear many Chinese parents prefer their children to marry Chinese.

Lowering her voice further this time, Jade quickly looks around. She whispers into my ear that she herself is *Han* Chinese, but her husband is *Hui*, a Chinese Muslim. Her husband considers that their daughter is Muslim by birth, therefore she should comply with the Muslim tradition to date a Muslim young man for marriage. I turn to look at Jade, who has just disclosed the secret racial and religious combination in her family.

I start to wonder why I had absolutely no idea that my next-door neighbours are a Chinese Muslim man married to a non-Muslim Chinese woman. Since both our families shop at T&T, a well-established chain of Chinese supermarkets, I have simply assumed that we eat the same kind of food. Now I taste bitterness. Looking at Jade, I am speechless. I don't know what to say or how to comfort her, as if I need time to be reassured that my next-door neighbours aren't much different from who I thought they were. Somehow, I feel her family discord is related to world disorder of the twenty-first century. Meanwhile, Jade looks at me earnestly, expecting me to say something. Finally, I managed to utter a few words, totally impersonal, "With tolerance, Canadians expect all neighbours of whatever religious beliefs or cultures to live together respectfully as law-abiding citizens. As parents, we should practice democracy with our children as we do in the broader Canadian society." I want to apologize to Jade for borrowing public discourse on such a family matter. I hear my words resonate the tone of political correctness.

The subway train pushes ahead, screeching at high speed. I draw a deep breath, hold it for a long minute or two, hoping the sharp noise would stop. While the hurtful noise continues, I feel a deep psychological scar from a half century ago suddenly becoming sensitive again. With an educated father who happened to have a brother in Taiwan, my family was deemed politically untrustworthy even before the Cultural Revolution in 1966. My junior high school deprived me of senior high school education. Years later, when I was in my earlier twenties, my employer, the railway bureau, blocked my career. This kind of discrimination was politically endorsed and socially reinforced. Individuals who belonged to the undesirable categories of families had to live out their fates, bearing the shame and suffering without public understanding or empathy.

Before the train enters our destination station, Jade lowers her voice one more time to a whisper, "His Muslim identity has gradually become a personal statement for my husband, especially in the years after 9/11." The train comes to a full stop, the door chime loudly disengages us from Jade's family story. We rush out. Instead of laughing giddily as we did half an hour before, we exhale loudly as if carrying a heavy burden.

Going home, we walk quietly. When we reach the back of our townhouses, I ask Jade, "Have you talked to your daughter since last Sunday night?"

"I talk to her every day, sometimes several times a day," she says, rubbing her eyes. "Today Silver asked me a strange question—whether her father had ever asked me to cover up my hair. He hasn't, I told my daughter honestly. But, he has asked me quite a few times to give him another child, a son. He says he desperately wants to have a son."

"Are you going to?" I am curious.

"Oh, no, absolutely not! I have given him a firm answer each time he brings it up." Jade smirks, "He should know I am already post-menopausal."

At that, we burst out laughing like two teenage schoolgirls sharing a joke about sex. "Congratulations! May you live in interesting times, according to the Chinese curse," I utter the English phrase, playfully.

"What? What's interesting?"

"Never mind." I realize the so-called Chinese curse only exists in English, it is impossible to explain the phrase in Chinese to a Chinese.

This past summer I had placed a large planter of scarlet red geraniums in the middle of our shared walkway. Today half a dozen flowers are blooming, some stems hanging over the brim of the planter. Jade bends down to touch a large flower. She says that there are no houseplants inside her house; even an aloe vera plant gradually died in her kitchen. I believe that is true. I have never seen any plants on their balcony.

Standing on the porch, Jade says her daughter laughed wildly upon hearing that her father desperately wants a son. The young woman says she would rather stay single for another decade to become a *Sheng Nu* [剩女, leftover woman], as the Chinese would say these days, than to date or marry someone who was her father's choice.

Opal

It has been three months since my dental appointment. I decided to call Opal, my hygienist, to fulfill my promise of meeting her for coffee before my next dental appointment. This will be the first time for us to meet outside the dentist's office. I am curious how she looks without her two-piece, solid colour uniform.

We have chosen a beautiful Sunday afternoon. After leaving my car at a parking lot, I step into a large social area with tables and chairs below a glass dome under the blue sky. What a lovely place Opal has found for us to share a moment of friendship! She walks toward me taking big strides. She is wearing black sports shorts, a typical red-white Canadian T-shirt, and matching running shoes.

"Hey, young lady," I greet her loudly, "you look radiant!"

She rushes over to give me a big hug. "My energy is overwhelming!" Indeed, her face is flushed. Tiny beads of sweat glisten on the tip of her nose and forehead.

"You look so much different outside of the dentist's office. What've you been doing the last three months?"

Her answer is quite simple. "I am extremely happy, Pearl."

Over a cup of Moroccan coffee, Opal starts to share her travelogue with me. She and a girlfriend had visited southern France in the summer. One of the places she visited is called Carcassonne, where she met an interesting guy who was also a runner.

"Hold on, you run your course too fast," I complain softly. "Instead of running a winding marathon, you hit the finish line right away."

"You are right!" Opal gets more excited. "How did you know we ran a marathon in France?"

"Did you? And with a young man?"

"Yes, I did! That's how I met him."

I sip my coffee to slow her down; following my example, she opens the lid of her coffee cup.

Her story began in the medieval town of Caunes-Minervois in southern France. One morning when she was starting her run, another runner, staying in the same hostel, came out. They started chatting and he told her he was running to the church of Notre

Dame du Cros. Its original chapel dated back to the seventh century.

"Can you believe it, he was also from Toronto?" she says. "His name was Jason."

It took them ten minutes to get out of the granite block lanes to the main road. It was a dirt road and there was almost no traffic. On their way they passed vineyards. The area was known for its wine, la Minervoise. Some wild apples and pears were hanging on trees beside the road, probably survivals of orchards that were replaced by the single grape crop.

After running for about five kilometres, they saw an old church with Roman arches, sitting in the basin of a green valley. Strikingly, on the roof of the church was a large bronze church bell and a metal cross.

"Oh, Pearl, now visualize this old parish church, sitting in the green valley and surrounded by rocky hills," Opal says dreamily.

"Mm," I close my eyes, "sounds like excellent Feng Shui for spiritual pursuit."

"That's right! The church is known for its healing and rejuvenating power," Opal confirms.

They were surprised to see many cars parked in front of the church. It turned out that that day, September 8, according to local legend, was Mary's birthday. Apparently, this church is one of the few Catholic churches in the world that still celebrates Mary's birthday.

Opal pauses, sips her coffee, and says in a mysterious voice, "And at that very moment, while the church bell was ringing at noon, with its sound bouncing up and down the valley, something was stirring inside me. Guess what?"

Following Opal's descriptions, I visualize the scene, the sun shining brightly at noon and the green valley vibrant with fertile energy.

"You felt energized," I respond enthusiastically.

"Yes, indeed, and more specifically, I felt a longing for my womanhood."

"Ah. How did that happen?"

They went inside the church. She went and stood under a small wooden sculpture of Mary holding baby Jesus, which has been on this original back wall of the church for centuries. She gazed at Mary for a very long moment and saw Mary smiling at her.

Opal mumbles, as if talking to herself, she wonders if Jason had also felt an intuitive longing for her, as she had for him that day. She says that day it didn't matter to her if Jason were younger than she, and she believes Mary must have lent the divine power to make it simple for them.

"What do you mean by simple?" I ask Opal softly.

She smiles, "No attachment."

"Still true?"

She hesitates, "Somewhat." They have been lovers since that day, as if there is no tomorrow, but still with no attachment.

The coffee has lasted for about an hour and before we say goodbye, Opal takes out a magazine from her knapsack, "Yours?"

It's the *Zoomer* magazine with Margaret Trudeau's photo on the cover.

"Oh, my goodness," I am bewildered. "How did you know I wanted to read this magazine?"

"I noticed it on the dentist's chair after you left last time. I knew it was yours, so I had it put away, here it is."

"It's not mine," I correct her. "I picked it up in your waiting room."

"Oh? But, it doesn't really matter. Do you still want it?"

"Of course!" I snatch it from her. "I really want to read it. Thank you for bringing it!"

"OK, crazy woman! Margaret Trudeau has lived an extraordinary life. Have fun with her story!"

Ruby

"I need your support, Pearl, can you help me?" A tearful, high-pitched, British voice sends a string of alarming signals to my ear through the telephone line.

"Are you all right, Ruby? Shall I call 911 for you? Do you want me to come over?" I ask, but receive no answers. I guess that Ruby is not physically injured or in any danger. This is not an emergency.

Ruby is a cheerful person, whose laughter rather than tears usually greet me on the phone. I rarely receive calls from her when she is not in a happy mood. Today she is definitely agitated; she sounds upset. As I go back to cooking my dinner, her story streams through the telephone line, an earful.

Ruby says she has terminated her decade-long relationship with her friend Gary. I notice she didn't say boyfriend. This decision, she says, was serious; she had been stressed for months. But now it has become too upsetting for her to face the consequences. That's why she has called me. She ends her sobbing with relief, saying, "See you tomorrow afternoon."

Putting the telephone receiver down on the kitchen counter, suddenly I remember I was grilling a piece of organic Norwegian salmon for dinner. It was supposed to be in the oven for only eight to ten minutes. Now I can smell burnt fish in the entire kitchen. Of course, it's my own fault for not switching off the oven when the phone rang. Now I am so annoyed I think I would need a drink to calm my nerves.

Fortunately, I don't drink; but I love nuts. I take out a variety of my favourite nuts and with a large mug of bitter rye herbal tea, and an apple, I sit down to eat an unusual but creative dinner.

I met Ruby a year ago at an Easter Sunday celebration organized by a new-age Christian church. The group didn't have its own church building, they rented the gymnasium of a downtown

Catholic College. Ruby and I were invited by our common friend Amber, a serious student of the Bible but not a member of an established church. Ruby is middle-aged, blond, and full-bodied. She had immediately impressed me by her enthusiasm when meeting a new friend. I liked her as soon as we were introduced.

"What part of China did you come from?" Ruby asked me immediately.

I was quite surprised, since this is usually the first question raised by fellow Chinese expatriates upon a first meeting. "Wuhan," I told her, waiting curiously to see why this would matter to her.

"I have been there," said Ruby, smiling and reminiscing, "the Yangtze River, the Yellow Crane Pagoda, and a legendary poet, who flew away riding the mythical yellow crane."

I was impressed. She said she had been to China twice by herself. The first trip was to northern China from Beijing to Xian and the Silk Road. During her second trip, she visited central and southern China, including Wuhan, Changsha, Guangzhou, and her favourite Chinese city of Guiling.

"Guiling is my favourite city as well!" I exclaimed. The distance between us two strangers was instantly shortened when we could share our travelogues in China. I started recalling my memories of Guiling. "Talking about Guiling, I actually sat on a bamboo raft drifting down the Li River on a summer afternoon!"

"Did you? I took the steam boat, which was the only transportation vehicle for the water route. But if I had known bamboo rafts were available, I definitely would have chosen it."

I didn't tell her that when hiring the bamboo raft, I was informed that I might need to jump off the raft at any time if a police patrol came within visible distance. In fact, I did jump into the shallow Li River three times during the ride. For an obvious, non-Chinese tourist like Ruby, I don't think any bamboo-raft owner would have taken her.

If caught, the owner would be charged not only for operating an illegal business, but also for potentially risking a foreign tourist's life. In addition to huge fines, the raft would be confiscated and destroyed. I didn't tell Ruby all this, so her memory of Guiling remains the same: serene blue sky, clear green Li River with a few bamboo rafts romantically and leisurely floating down the river. From time to time, the bamboo raft owners sing folk songs, while a few water buffalo cool themselves in the shallow water, keeping their noses above the water. It is truly picturesque like in a painting.

Shortly after we met, I invited Ruby to an Asian Heritage Month event in which I would participate at the Aga Khan Museum. She asked me if she could get a ride with me on the day. Of course, I was delighted, appreciating her prompt commitment, including spending an extra half day with me preparing for the event.

The afternoon event featured Taoism and Sufism. My group of artists delivered a multimedia stage production of Taoism, Tai Chi, and meditation. Half way through, we invited ten volunteers from the audience to the stage. Ruby rose up from her seat in the middle of the auditorium and came forward.

Later that day, we watched Sufi dance in the outdoor courtyard. I was completely mesmerized by the spinning movements of the male dancers wearing unique white outfits and tall hats. It was a challenging sight, visually and culturally. I was preoccupied by some haunting questions—what kind of milieu would produce these male whirling dancers? What is the ultimate goal of the spinning movement? Eventually, the hour-long performance ended, the crowd dispersed and the musicians and dancers began collecting their instruments and rolling up their carpets. Standing in the courtyard in a trance, head spinning with even more questions, I saw Ruby chatting with one of the dancers. I wanted to walk over with my own questions, but I hesitated, unsure whether I would offend the dancer.

Later, sitting in my car, Ruby shared with me that the Sufi dance originated in Turkey in the twelfth century. The dancers spin until they feel spiritually connected to God. The dancer whom she had talked to had told her that Sufi dance could also be a form of meditation to lose one's ego in order to be connected with the divine through a mysterious intoxicating journey.

Ruby continued to elaborate about similar dances in Egypt which she had seen during her travels. According to her, the Egyptian costumes are more colourful, though the spinning is similar. "What about the spinning movements in contemporary dance?" I asked. "Is it somehow related to the tradition of Sufi dance?"

"I don't know." She admitted that she was neither an expert on ancient religious dances, nor on contemporary ones. In fact, she was not a specialist in any field. "But whenever I am curious about something, I just ask questions. That's all." She looked at me with a simple smile, shrugging her shoulders.

Since then I have known Ruby for two years.

Within twenty hours after receiving Ruby's panic call pleading for my support, I am pressing the buzzer of her condominium apartment. I have made it for two o'clock sharp as we agreed. Stepping out of the elevator, I see her apartment just opposite the elevator.

"Hello, how are you today?" I greet Ruby, who is standing outside the door frame. Before I have a chance to give her a hug, my eyes are drawn toward a famous Qing Dynasty Chinese brush painting on her wall.

"Where did you get this painting?" I ask her earnestly. "Oh, I mean the print," I walk inside her apartment toward the painting, forgetting to take off my outdoor shoes.

"I bought it in Beijing."

"Do you know the painter was not Chinese?"

"That's right! He was an Italian artist, a Jesuit missionary sent to China in the seventeenth century. He was hired officially by the Qing Dynasty emperors to be their court artist." Ruby smiles at me, a proud, well-informed owner of the reproduction.

"Yes, indeed," I add cheerfully. "I am so impressed by your knowledge, Lady Ruby. The artist also painted the emperors' portraits, horses and dogs. By the way, one more question, do you happen to know his name?"

"Of course," Ruby continues as a charming hostess with great manners, knowledge, and sophistication, as if she were giving me a grand tour of an ancient castle in Europe. "His Italian name was, let me see, I've got it somewhere in my head. Giuseppe Castiglione? Is it? I believe it is." She nods at me, smiling. "Now, my honoured guest, Lady Pearl, would you be so kind as to tell me the painter's Chinese name?"

I knew it was Emperor Qianglong of the Qing Dynasty who had chosen Castiglione for his court artist and bestowed on him a Chinese name. The name is always at the tip of my tongue. He was a very famous and most productive European artist, who had adopted Chinese art media and combined it with certain European painting techniques in his artistic practice. He had spent his entire adult life as a court artist for different emperors of the Qing Dynasty, and eventually died of old age in Beijing. Now that we are talking about him, I can visualize one of his famous paintings, *One Hundred Horses*, but somehow, I am tongue-tied for the moment, unable to pronounce his Chinese name. Searching through my mind for an intense minute, and holding my breath, suddenly, the artist's name pops up. "Lang-Shi-Ning, yes, it's Lang Shining!" I repeat the three characters, while I visualize the physical shapes of the Chinese characters one by one.

But I have lost Ruby's attention after dawdling too long on the painter's Chinese name. When we finally sit down on the couch in her sitting room, Ruby has changed the subject of the conversation altogether. "I want to ask you about something else, Pearl, it's personal, if you don't mind."

"No, not at all, please go ahead," I tell her.

"Have you ever tried online dating?"

"What? Do you mean internet dating? No, I haven't." I am quite surprised at her question. It suddenly makes me feel out of touch with current trends, as if I were being asked by a teenager about a new computer game.

"Why not?" She inquires expectantly.

"Mm, a good question. I haven't sensed the need, I suppose . . . overall, I am too busy to expand my social life. Plus, I don't know how to handle popularity, in case suddenly I became hot in cyber space, I wouldn't know how to handle that." Laughing at the funny idea I ask Ruby, "What about you?"

"Yes, I have. About a year ago, I signed up with an online dating company. I wanted to meet some interesting men," she confesses honestly.

"I see. So have you met any interesting men yet?"

"Yes, you bet. Are you ready?" Ruby winks at me mischievously.

I lean back on the couch, waiting to be entertained.

Several weeks after Ruby signed up with a reputable internet dating website, the agency informed her that they had found a true gentleman for her to meet. The gentleman had expressed interest in Ruby's profile. The meeting was arranged at a Starbucks in the west end of the city, not too far from Ruby's home. In fact, said the agent, the gentleman lived in the same area. How convenient! Good luck to you both!

When Ruby walked into the coffee shop for the date, she

immediately spotted a white-haired gentleman with square shoulders sitting at a table facing the entrance, with a serious expression on his face. He stood up as soon as he identified Ruby with the picture from the dating site. Their hands touched, they sat down awkwardly, face to face, to start a conversation. During the next ten minutes, Ruby had answered more than a dozen questions from the intended boyfriend. Suddenly, she realized that she hadn't come to her first date to be interrogated by a stranger. She was expecting a courteous, friendly conversation over a cup of cappuccino and find out a bit about this man, while revealing something about herself. She stood up, apologized to the man and quickly left the place.

"That was my first date. What do you think?" Ruby pauses, expecting my comments. I come up with none, and she says, "The next day, the agent phoned to tell me that the gentleman I had met was a retired court judge!"

I can't help but burst out laughing at this. "Did his worship give you an endorsement?"

"Endorsement? Yes, apparently, he did," Ruby chuckles. "I am not joking. His worship is interested in another meeting. I simply requested the agency match me with men of my age or younger."

"Oh, yeah, that will work for you. Have you met any energetic, youthful, more interesting retirees after that?" I laugh at my own idealistic description of male candidates for energetic female retirees like Ruby.

Ruby exhaled a deep sigh, averting her eyes to the floor with emotionally restrained reticence. The fire in her witty eyes flicks and then dims like a tealight candle burning up its candle wax in a small container. I observe my friend more closely. She appears to be aging fast, her face and neck seem paler and wrinkled. In order not to disturb her in this moment of self-absorbed silence, I look around the room. There are decorative flowers on the surfaces of all her furniture. On the desk, the dining room table, the kitchen counter, and the coffee table in front of us, there is exactly the same kind of woven basket with artificial pink roses. I draw a deep breath and wait. Finally Ruby wipes her tears silently with a tissue and murmurs without looking at me, "I haven't had another date since then." The agent explained to her that men liked to meet with women at least ten years younger than themselves. The agent couldn't find another man willing to meet with her except the retired judge, who was still waiting and hoping to see her again.

I feel ever more sympathetic with Ruby when she shares the statistics of single women registered for online dating. According to the agent, men have a lot more choices, including foreign women, who may not even speak fluent English. Some of the women, in fact, are well educated and financially independent. There are many pretty young women from Russia, Ukraine and China on the dating websites. Typically, the Chinese women are from their mid-thirties to early forties. In North America, we would definitely consider them young women, unfortunately, in China, their own compatriots call them Leftover Women. Now, with internet dating services, single Chinese women can seek marriage-minded Canadian and American men. In the domestic pool, Ruby learned, men want to meet divorced career women, with or without young children. The agent gave Ruby his final analysis, saying, "It is very rare that a gentleman takes an interest in an old spinster."

"No!" I scream out. My inner peace has been savaged by the old English phrase delivered clearly and cruelly by the dating agent.

"Are you OK?" Ruby asks.

I shake my head. "English dictionary," I say, stretching out my hand to her. She passes me her dictionary without delay. "Now, read the history of the word," I tell her, passing the opened dictionary back to Ruby. She starts to read.

"The development of the word spinster is a good example of the way in which a word acquires strong connotations to the extent that it can no longer be used in a neutral sense." She pauses to look at me. "Go on," I ask her seriously.

She continues, "From the seventeenth century the word was appended to names as the official legal description of an unmarried woman: Elizabeth Harris of London, spinster. This usage survives today in some legal and religious contexts. In modern usage, however, spinster is a derogatory term, referring or alluding to the stereotype of an older woman who is unmarried, childless, prissy, and repressed."

Putting down the dictionary, Ruby looks at me.

"I would like to hear the dating agent apologize to you for using that derogatory word," I suggest to Ruby. "Would you like me to call and tell him you are an independent career woman, an adventurous solo world traveller, a proud property owner, and a retired schoolteacher with financial independence? You would like him to profile you in such terms when he introduces you to men of your age or younger."

"Yes," Ruby smiles, "I like your description of me, thank you, Pearl."

We dial the online dating agency. I speak briefly with the dating agent about how the word *spinster* discriminates against single women like us with a three-hundred-year-old gender stereotype. I pass the phone to Ruby, the agent apologizes sincerely to her, promising to be more sensitive to single, unmarried women. Restating her profile, Ruby asks the agent to introduce her as how she sees herself. The agent answers, "Absolutely!"

A smile appears on Ruby's face. After a long pause, with her hands holding mine, Ruby asks me carefully, looking seriously concerned, "By the way, how do you say 'Leftover Women' in Chinese?"

"*Sheng Nu*," I give her the pronunciation in Mandarin.

"It sounds like spinster, name-calling."

I remember the Nobel Peace Prize winner, Desmond Tutu observing that in our surviving genes, human beings are intuitively connected to mirror each other's experiences.

For the remaining afternoon, Ruby suggests we take a walk for fresh air in High Park, which is only five minutes away from her condo. As soon as she mentions the outdoors, the air in her unit smells thick and stale. I look around, there is a small balcony, but its entrance had been blocked. All the windows are locked and covered with thick, floor-length, navy-blue, double-lined draperies. I am more than ready to leave this bird-cage of an apartment.

Jade

On an early evening in the beautiful fall season, after working for a whole day on the computer, I look forward to a rejuvenating walk by the lake. I step out of the back door of my townhouse, while my neighbours' brand-new black Chevrolet drives into the laneway in golden sunset. Jade steps out with two bags of groceries and her husband, Tie Sheng, emerges from the driver's side carrying more shopping bags.

"Hey, Pearl, going out?" the couple greet me almost simultaneously.

"Can I help you with some bags?"

"We're OK, Tie Sheng is just dropping off the bags, then he is leaving for the night shift right away," says Jade. "Pearl, I am not working tonight, do you want to come over later? Let's make vegetable *baozi* for dinner."

"Vegetable *baozi*! My favourite!" I am delighted to accept her invitation.

An hour later, with twilight descending, a solar-powered

streetlight penetrates the misty atmosphere in our back lane. I look forward to *baozi* made with fresh dough, sesame oil, and mixed vegetables. I call Jade to report my availability.

"Come over and watch me make *baozi*!"

Jade's kitchen is as cluttered as mine. While mine is full of paper and files on the table as in an ill-managed office, hers looks like a disorganized warehouse exhibiting various types of food. On the kitchen floor, in shopping bags, are mounds of fresh vegetables that they bought this afternoon. On top of the kitchen counter are dried seafood and mushrooms in opened packages as well as Chinese turnip, nicknamed white radish in English, preserved inside large glass jars in hot chili sauce. On the other side of the kitchen are opened or unfinished boxes of cookies, donuts, and special sweets from different special occasions.

There are more bags on top of a square table next to the counter. I can see a large package of all-purpose flour for making the fermented dough for *baozi*. Jade, with her sleeves rolled up to her elbows, in a loose housecoat and a pair of plastic slippers, fits perfectly into her messy kitchen. As her next-door neighbour, I also feel comfortable in her homey kitchen, awaiting her homemade specialty.

An extra-large, stainless steel bowl sits on the counter. Jade, with a pair of kitchen scissors, is swiftly cutting bean sprouts into the huge bowl. Periodically, she mixes in other ingredients using long chopsticks. I realize that the *baozi* my mouth was salivating for has yet to be made, and the smell of freshly steamed dough was merely an illusion created by my brain from past memory. I utter a silent sigh. Now, while waiting, I have an important task to complete. Ever since our unexpected encounter on the subway train more than a month ago, I have been waiting for another opportunity to chat with Jade. This lucky evening has brought me a rare opportunity to be alone with her in her kitchen.

I ask her why she decided to make *baozi* tonight. She throws me an incredulous look. "To eat, of course. Tie Sheng needs to take food with him on the night shift every day. When there is nothing in the fridge, he just buys junk food." Jade points to the box of donuts on the side table. I realize that she cares a great deal about what her husband eats.

"You know T&T Supermarket sells fresh *baozi*," I inform her.

"I know," she responds quickly. "Tie Sheng sometimes buys a few packages, but they don't taste good with the thick dough and little filling. Too expensive too, six dollars for six *baozi* plus HST, too much."

"What're your ingredients?" Standing on the opposite side of the kitchen counter, I can't tell exactly what is inside the huge stainless-steel bowl, which is almost full to the brim. Jade starts to tell me her recipe, as she continues stirring and mixing the ingredients. "Korean mushrooms, Chinese wood-ear black mushrooms, Canadian white mushrooms, green onion, mung bean sprouts, coriander, a pack of chopped-up firm tofu sheets, tiny dried shrimp with the shells on, five eggs scrambled and minced, and then I will add some vegetable oil, a teaspoon of salt, and some ground black pepper."

"My goodness, what a list! How many *baozi* can you make with this much filling?"

"About fifty, medium size."

"That's fifty dollars saved, it beats T&T *baozi*!" I exclaim. "Of course, more nutritious and better taste. You know what, maybe you should start a *baozi* business."

"Oh yeah, Tie Sheng would sit at home and eat *baozi* all day long," Jade says with a laugh. "I bet you he can eat ten of them in one meal," she adds with a smile.

I smile back at her. "That makes sense, since you are a great *baozi* chef, he has to be an outstanding *baozi* eater so as not to disappoint you."

"What?" Jade says, puzzled. Realizing I am teasing her, she lets out a deep sigh. "I wish he knew how lucky he is to have a wife like me. After working a twelve-hour shift, I decided to make *baozi* from scratch, simply because he said he misses homemade *baozi*."

As we chat away, Jade is busy rolling the dough into small flat pieces, then putting mixed vegetables in the centre of each piece. She pulls up the edges of the dough and wraps up in pleats to make a perfect *baozi*. She explains that she needs to leave the finished raw *baozi* on a wooden cutting board for a half hour to allow the yeast to rise. Later when she is ready to steam them, she places eight on a rack inside the steamer, which is sitting on the stove. Soon I can smell the aroma of fresh steamed dough as it gradually permeates the entire kitchen. My mouth is watering by real experience this time. Jade finally turns off the heat and dramatically lifts the lid of the steamer. Behind the rising steam I see eight chubby, puffy white *baozi* leaning against each other. Once in contact with the cool air, they start to shrink in front of our eyes, and wrinkles form on their skins.

"Bravo!" I cheer her success, but Jade says critically, "If we let them sit a bit longer before steaming, they could puff up even more."

Finally, it's time to taste the *baozi*. She picks up a *baozi* with her hand and places it on my plate.

It's delicious. I know I will never find this quality in any of the restaurant or supermarket brands.

Shortly after I finish my first *baozi*, I steer our conversation towards her family. "I notice your husband has changed recently."

"How so?" Jade looks amused.

"He's shaved his beard. I just noticed it today. He looks much younger."

"Oh, his beard—I'm surprised too," she says. "He was growing his beard for the last six months, but I didn't make a fuss, just left him alone. Now he's gotten rid of it, but it was his own decision."

"How is his relationship with your daughter?" I ask.

"Improved, somewhat. He's too stubborn to apologize to the girl or to shake hands with her boyfriend, but at least his attitude has softened. Last Saturday night when the boyfriend dropped off Silver, Tie Sheng took a diet Cola from the fridge for Silver to pass to her young man."

"That's a nice gesture. I am sure he wants to hold onto his family for all the *baozi* his wife will be making in the future. And he would want to be the proud father at his daughter's graduation." I see an 18 by 18 inch framed photo on the wall with a glamorous picture of Silver.

"This is my third now, it's addictive," I confess to her, biting into another fresh *baozi*. Jade smiles. I don't know what she thinks of me—a single woman in her sixties, a next-door neighbour for almost ten years, whom she has just started to socialize with after an accidental encounter on a subway train. Why should she trust me with her family secrets?

By now hot moisture from the steamer fills the entire kitchen. Every fifteen minutes another set of hot, puffy *baozi* is ready. Our conversation drifts freely in both directions. She asks me why I didn't get remarried when I was younger and more attractive. I laugh, recalling that once her husband gave me the same advice when we were both coming out of our garages and met at the back door landing.

After a while Jade pulls her chair closer to me, a *baozi* in her hand. "I have some news to tell you," she says.

I don't know what to expect this time. The night is growing old, and we have been chatting for three hours in her kitchen.

"I bought that house in North York," she says and waits for my response. I remember that when we were sitting in the subway, she mentioned she wanted to move out and live by herself. She actually showed me a printout describing a detached house for sale.

"You did? Are you serious about moving out?" I am concerned for her, while she looks too calm. I can't believe that she is at the stage of considering a separation from her husband.

"How much did you pay for this house?" I ask.

"1.8 million," she says gently without raising the tone of her voice, but she has certainly raised my blood pressure. I try to sit still, not showing my concern. Jade, a new immigrant, a nurse, alone, has bought a luxury home priced at 1.8 million for herself! I ask her calmly, "When is the closing date? Do you have a moving date yet?"

"We are not moving." She answers softly, delivering the punchline of an unfunny joke.

"What? We? You bought the new house with your husband?" I've raised my voice.

"Yes." The expression in her eyes now shocks me more than the 1.8 million price tag.

The husband and wife have bought the 1.8-million property as a joint investment!

"The real estate agent predicts the house value will appreciate to pass two million next spring. We will sell it then and make a $200, 000 profit."

I am speechless.

It is nearly midnight when I finally get back to my own kitchen on the other side of the wall. Jade has given me six *baozi* to take home. A full moon shines high in the sky, cool silver moonlight flooding through the double sliding glass doors to the kitchen floor. Sitting in the cool moonlight, I eat two more *baozi*, absentmindedly. There is no doubt that I have become addicted to Jade's ingredients.

Pearl

While the moon is moving slowly towards the east, I switch the kitchen lights on, contemplating a cup of *Pu Er* tea before going to bed. Blinking my sleepy eyes, I glance across the messy kitchen, my all-purpose workstation, the centre of my daily life. A patch of bright red colour on top of a pile of books catches my attention. I am surprised, but not really alarmed, to see that it is the long-waiting *Zoomer* magazine with Margaret Trudeau's photo on the cover.

"My goodness! I can't believe it!" I exclaim to myself.

"Of course," I soften my tone to correct the unapologetic statement. "Of course, I can definitely believe this." Day in day out, I work on my computer to meet various deadlines. I eat my three meals and drink my coffee and tea here, surrounded by cables and papers. I can't clearly distinguish how each particular object relates to the passage of time, or whether they are meaningful in the phenomenal progress of my life and personal growth. Perhaps, tonight, right now, in between night and day, darkness and light, *yin* and *yang*, I will claim one extraordinary moment for myself.

I clear two square feet of space on the surface of the workstation, then I sit down at the table. I start to read the magnificent life of Margaret Trudeau. It is actually a long article based on an interview. Margaret Trudeau's five decades of exciting, happy and sad life spreads out in the magazine pages. It takes me an hour to reach the last page, where the writer shares her interviewee's ultimate realization with the readers without any hesitation or reservation:

If Margaret Trudeau could go back and tell her younger self one thing, it would be this: "I wish I'd known that being me was going to be all right," she says. "That I would be allowed to be me, holding onto my own quirky self, my own ideas. That I'd have to fight hard to be me. But I would make it."

Sipping my cup of warm *Pu Er*, I taste its rich suppleness instead of just quenching my usual thirst, and a realization gradually dawns on me. After four decades, I finally exhale a deep sigh to disconnect myself from an emotional burden. I do not need to justify or to explain to others why I have chosen to remain single ever since I divorced an abusive husband in my mid-twenties in China. It's hard for me to believe that the new Chinese slang, *sheng nu*, or Leftover Woman, has been coined officially and discriminatively to categorize millions of educated Chinese women in Mainland China who have chosen to remain single. Are young Chinese women not burdened by the same fears that Margaret Trudeau identified in her interview? Perhaps they have transformed the fears inherited from their mothers and grandmothers into courage and strength. As a celebrity, Margaret Trudeau's self-realization surprisingly mirrors the passage of life shared by ordinary women. We should all be more confident and accept our true selves.

Sipping my tea, I smile, recalling how miraculously the magazine has followed me from the dentist's office to my kitchen on a cool moonlit night. And tonight I sensed an urgency to read it for the first time. Perhaps, I should send a copy to other women, maybe to Ruby first. Perhaps, it will inspire her to reflect on her own wondrous life, and celebrate it with her friends.

Ruby

Ever since I visited Ruby concerning her personal crisis, I have been dodging her many telephone calls. Recently she started calling me multiple times every day from nine am to nine pm, her bedtime. There seems no particular reason for her calls other than to deliver a warmhearted greeting or an appreciation of the photos I have taken of her. Sometimes she greets me by another woman's name; I laugh at it without making a fuss to correct her mistake.

It seems to me she has a list of friends to call, like a telemarketer. Finally, after a few consecutive days of more than three calls, I let the telephone ring and let her leave a message. It's a boring job for me to delete all her messages. I don't even bother to listen to them anymore, assuming they must all be the same.

After adopting this temporary solution for a few weeks, I wonder whether I have been unfair to Ruby. Why can't friends call each other just to say hello? Of course, that's exactly what most of us do for Christmas, Chinese New Year, birthdays and so on, to renew our friendships. But there is a fine line between friends, otherwise a friend could become a nuisance.

Trying to find a solution, I casually talk to Ruby about the interesting features of smart cellphones. Instead of dialing up my friends one by one for the same holiday greetings, I can send out one text message with a cute emoji sticker in a couple of minutes. This appears to be the most efficient way to stay in touch with distant relatives, friends, and old colleagues. But I get into an argument with Ruby, when she insists that she is too smart to waste her money on a smartphone.

"Of course, you do. Instead of ringing people daily on your home line, interrupting them, you can send a text message with a nice graphic cartoon icon."

Ruby disagrees, saying that getting a smartphone means extra costs. I change my focus: "As a professional single woman with financial independence, you definitely need a smartphone, for mobile use, for personal safety, for business contacts, and in your case, for potential romantic relationships. By the way, are you still looking forward to meeting interesting men online? How do you expect them to reach you?"

"I would like them to leave messages on my home answering machine, so I can listen to them when I get home," answers Ruby logically. "I won't miss any calls."

I don't understand why she is so adamant about a smartphone. At the same time, I can only laugh at myself for making great efforts in vain to help a friend manage her social life. While looking for a manageable, mutually enjoyable way to spend time with Ruby, I remember she had mentioned once that she enjoys live theatre and art galleries. I think I may have a more effective approach to help her break her addiction to calling people. I deliver my proposal to her the next time she calls.

"What about booking a couple of operas for the fall season? We will have some regular entertainment on the calendar and we can get together then." Ruby is excited but then expresses a concern, "In the old days, Gary and I used to go out on Friday evenings for dinner and then to live theatre. After a while, he said it was too expensive."

"Hey listen, Ruby, we are not inviting Gary to go out with us. I thought you had stopped seeing him—haven't you?" I remember that Ruby's latest emotional crisis was triggered by her breakup with Gary. She had then signed up with an online dating website. "Now listen, just you and I, two women going to the opera."

Ruby is quiet, and I figure she must be thinking about what it means to be going out with a woman friend. She is silent. I realize I must quickly deliver the entire proposal to Ruby before my own enthusiasm loses its momentum. So I suggest we pick three shows and choose the best seats in Ring 5 for an incredible price of $200.

After asking me a few relevant questions, Ruby agrees to my proposal, so we will see each other in the fall while going to the operas. Crossing my fingers, I hope this new plan will reset Ruby's anxiety button. In fact, she starts to call me once a day, in the morning only, to which I respond attentively for a few minutes.

Our daily telephone conversation continues throughout the summer, building up an intense expectation for the forthcoming first opera in September. On the actual evening, I arrive at the

Four Seasons Centre at 6:30 pm sharp and I am delighted to see Ruby outside waiting for me. She wears a long floral summer dress as it is quite warm in early fall, and I am wearing a short skirt and jacket. In my handbag, I have wrapped some cashews and grapes in facial tissues. In case Ruby gets hungry, we won't need to come down from Ring 5 to Ring 3 to buy a beverage or a snack. As her companion, I voluntarily give up my habit of taking the stairs, so Ruby and I squeeze into the elevator crowded with seniors and their walkers, and we reach the top floor without sweating.

Our seats are in the centre of the front row without anybody blocking our view. Our timing is excellent with ten minutes to read the program before curtain time. I lean back in my seat, expecting to enjoy an evening of live music and performance with my friend Ruby for the first time. But five minutes before show time, when I remember to put my cell phone on silent, Ruby stands up from her seat. Grabbing her jacket and handbag, she starts to squeeze out of our row and walks firmly toward the far back of the theatre.

"Ruby! Where are you going?" I yell at her from my seat. An usher, standing at the entrance to Ring 5 with a pile of programs in her hands, responds. "Excuse me! Excuse me!" she calls after Ruby. Some audience members stand up to see what has happened, causing further commotion on the floor. Ruby continues to walk up until she reaches the last row. She sits down on a seat and places her belongings on the empty seat beside her. By then the usher has caught up with her, though I cannot hear their conversation. Lights start to dim and then turn off. The usher leaves Ruby where she has chosen to sit. In fact, she is the only person sitting in the last row.

I shake my head and sigh. I simply cannot concentrate on the performance on the stage. I keep looking back to check the last row. It is too dark for me to see if Ruby is still sitting there. In the end, I tell myself, Ruby is an adult and she should be able to look after herself.

At intermission I am relieved to see Ruby still sitting up there by herself as if she were a queen, Her Royal Highness sitting on her royal throne. When I wave at her, she stands up and proceeds to come down. A couple of steps down, she pauses to talk to two men, one older than the other, and then to the usher, who was chasing after her before the show started. I assume she has no need for the washroom, or water from the fountain, so I step outside without waiting for her. Ten minutes later, Ruby comes into the lobby, looking for me. Finally, when we sit down on a bench beside the staircase, I ask her, "So what is your problem?"

"I don't feel safe sitting in the front row. I felt I was going to tip over the balcony. I always need to have at least one row of people in front of me. If I tip over, I would fall on top of them." I fix my gaze on her face, listening to her, before uttering my ultimate non-sense-intolerant response, "What—are—you—talking—about?"

"Besides, you know me," Ruby continues with a faint smile. "I enjoy talking to strangers. The two women sitting in front of me were very supportive. I know they wouldn't mind if I fall on top of them."

What total nonsense! She doesn't know what she has put me through. I sigh heavily. Do I mind coming to the opera with someone who is psychologically unstable? Someone who changes her seat without asking anyone? It bothers me, but if it will make her feel safer, and as long as there are empty seats available, I am willing to accept her decision and the usher on duty agrees. And I don't even mind if she talks nonsense to half a dozen strangers. But Ruby's last sentence, like a sharp knife, slashes open the thin layer of mutual respect between us. Suddenly I realize that my intention to involve a friend in activities of my own interest, hoping to find common ground for our friendship, is self-centered. No wonder it has failed miserably on our first night out. Perhaps what Ruby really enjoys is to meet strangers and get their attention for a few minutes rather than spend an evening with a dull friend like me. I remember how, two years ago, when we first met as total strangers on Easter Sunday, Ruby and I were engaged in a very long conversation about her trips to China and other parts of the world. As a result, we had completely ignored our common friend Amber. Did we offend Amber? Of course we did, and I apologized to Amber afterwards. As Ruby's companion at the opera, I didn't mind sitting by myself, but I cared to know why she suddenly left the seat beside me. Now it became clearer to me that I have misunderstood Ruby. After the intermission, I let go of my anxiety, hoping that we would now enjoy the rest of the opera. Nonetheless, I can't dismiss the thought of Ruby's abnormal behaviour. It may only be the tip of an iceberg, her mental status. I recall her small balcony that is blocked in her apartment. Is she afraid of heights? I purchased the expensive seats in the front row for us without knowing that Ruby preferred to sit in the last row.

The wake-up call comes a little too late. Ruby and I have booked two shows at the Mirvish Theatre. On an October evening, I am standing outside of the Princess of Wales Theatre at 7:20 pm sharp, but there is no sign of Ruby. Holding two tickets in my hand, I join a dozen men and women on the sidewalk waiting for theatre companions. I know that I should not worry too much since there are still forty minutes to show time. A pretty Asian woman stands beside me in a navy-blue miniskirt, black stockings, and knee-high black leather boots, looking enviously youthful and fashionable. Her companion is a handsome, well-groomed Black man. Most of the theatre audience consists of white-haired senior couples, but the Mirvish production has definitely attracted some youthful audience. A yellow Beck Taxi stops at the curb to let out an older couple with canes.

Standing near me on the sidewalk, a young woman is talking on the phone. I can overhear part of her conversation. She is talking to her mother, who has just come out of the St Andrew Subway station. "It takes less than ten minutes to walk from the subway to the Princess of Wales Theatre. Walk west, pass the Royal Alexandra Theatre, and continue on for a few minutes, and I'll be looking out for you!" She steps out to the edge of the sidewalk to wait for her mother. I envy her for the timely connection with her mother via their mobile phones. Within half an hour, I have witnessed a number of reunions on the sidewalk before the parties joyfully disappear into the theatre.

It starts to rain. I step back intuitively under the canopy. It's 7:40 pm already and no Ruby. Why isn't she equipped with a cell phone like everyone else? I start to question if an undiagnosed age-related illness is quietly taking control of her brain.

Another ten minutes slip by. I watch the rain splash mercilessly on the sidewalk and pedestrians jumping in and out of puddles in their expensive shoes.

Finally, it's time for me to check in and find my seat, when an old Chinese saying pops into my mind: "It is going to rain if your mother decides to marry another man." It ridicules people who fail to see when odd things happen. However, the last thing I must do in this odd situation is to dial Ruby's home number and leave her a full report of what I have done. I will leave her ticket in the pickup box window in case she shows up. My message will not alter whatever awkward situation she has gotten herself into, but it may help later to process what has happened this evening. That is if she cares to find out. As her friend, I have kept my promise to the last minute.

Three days after missing the show, Ruby finally calls. "I just want to let you know," she comes straight to the point without delivering her usual warm greetings. "I went downtown two times that day, but I didn't see you. I felt quite sick the second time, so I called Gary to come and take me home."

"Where in downtown did you go?" I ask.

"The theatre."

"Which theatre? Did you make sure it was the Princess of Wales Theatre?"

"I *don't* know!" She breaks down, starts to cry. She manages to deliver some details about that evening. "I asked people for directions when I got out of St Andrew Subway. And I followed the directions to the theatre. You were not there." Abruptly, the line gets cut off. Did Ruby hang up? This is a crucial moment when I can almost visualize what has happened that night. I just need to ask her one important question before unwrapping the riddle.

I ring her back immediately. I pray that she will pick up my call. She actually does, though she hasn't stopped sobbing. I take the opportunity to state my analysis as quickly as I can, "You probably didn't walk far enough to get to the Princess of Wales Theatre. You were probably waiting at the Royal Alex Theatre instead!"

"I have a severe headache right now. I *don't* want to talk about this anymore." Her voice fades.

"Ruby—please don't hang up, please," I beg her. "Just one last question. When you were waiting for me, did you see a super large theatre seat on the sidewalk?" I can hear her thinking since she hasn't hung up on me. There is a pause, during which she blows her nose, before she comes back to the receiver. "Yes, I was standing in front of the big Red Seat on the sidewalk, but you were not there." She hangs up.

Now I feel apologetic. Why didn't it occur to me that she might be waiting at the other theatre within a stone's throw of me. Even when I overheard the daughter directing her mother to walk past the Royal Alex before arriving at the Princess of Wales, it didn't occur to me that Ruby might make that mistake. I could have walked over to the Royal Alex to see if Ruby was waiting for me there. We could have come back together to the Princess of Wales before curtain time. Of course, if she was equipped with a smartphone, all this trouble could have been avoided.

After that incident, it seems that Ruby and I both have chosen not to get together any more. Like birds, maybe each of us needs to distance from the other in order to fly free and perhaps, fly farther and higher. Ruby has quit calling me, which I appreciate. After being left alone to my own routines, I find time to practice Tai Chi in the morning and take walks in the afternoon. I continue to go solo to theatres and operas as I used to before I met Ruby. Ruby and I have faded completely from each other's lives.

In early December, I sit down to write some annual Christmas cards to old friends. I enclose two theatre tickets inside the card for Ruby. They are for a popular holiday musical. The seats are just right for Ruby. On Christmas Eve, I will attend my friend Amber's annual holiday potluck dinner for single men and women. Each year we share tasty potluck dishes and sweets from multiple origins in the world, which have been brought over to Canada by generations of immigrants and refugees. The group has another annual holiday custom, we sing Christmas carols after dinner. Those who don't know the lyrics will simply hum or mumble along joyfully with the crowd. At eleven pm we will all go to St Paul's Cathedral on Bloor Street East to attend Midnight Mass under the glorious Gothic dome. We always look forward to it.

Spiritual Pursuits

They met at the Aga Khan Museum in early spring. None of them had ever been inside the Islamic cultural museum before. However, driving on the Don Valley Parkway, Linda has long been impressed by the white architecture, its roof rising above the busy highway. The combination of basic geometric lines and hexagonal shapes gives the building a serene, peaceful look under the blue sky. Now walking towards the museum, Linda was delighted to see in the vicinity another outstanding architecture with a pyramidal dome. The two buildings create a synergic architectural impact that Linda appreciates.

Inside the museum, Linda, Harry, and Andy found each other at the information desk. Standing in a triangular space, they talked continuously with each other for an hour without shifting from the spot underneath their feet. Attracted to each other by an invisible mysterious energy, they decided to meet again soon to form a meditation group for spiritual pursuits.

A week after the first April shower, Linda and Andy came to Markham Village. Walking on the damp soil, roots stirring underneath, they arrived at the corner lot. Harry opened the front door to welcome his new friends, offering them a studio tour as the starting point of their gathering.

"I teach private art students," said Harry, switching on the florescent lights as they descended down the stairs to the basement. Framed artworks were displayed on the walls, pencil sketches, pastel crayon drawings, acrylic and oil on canvas as well as Chinese ink brushwork on *Xuan* paper. Going through the studio, the host talked proudly about his students. "This young man is now a third-year fine art student at the Ontario College of Arts. The piece on my wall here was the original work he had submitted to OCA for admission." The guests stared at a large rectangular frame: numerous pieces of broken mirror were glued inside the frame to make it look like a completed jigsaw puzzle.

"A broken mirror?" Andy asked suspiciously. "And you call it art?"

Harry didn't explain. To Linda, it seemed that the student intended to save the aftermath of an accident that had shattered the mirror. All the broken pieces had been carefully relocated and glued back in place; the student had definitely created a psychological effect.

Ascending back to the ground floor, the group entered an open-concept area for cooking and dining. Three large terracotta mugs of different designs were lined up on the kitchen counter. "Shall we meditate first before having tea?" inquired the host. With no objection, the guests agreed that meditation was the original purpose of their gathering.

Now they entered a small room adjacent to the hallway. Calligraphy and abstract ink paintings decorated the walls, creating an atmosphere of tranquility. A few meditation cushions were scattered on the floor. They sat down, adjusting their sitting positions to form a triangle in order to share each other's energy. The men sat down in a half lotus position with their legs bending inward. Linda apologized for having injured her left knee in the past, so she sat down with her back straight and stomach tucked in. Andy set his iPhone for thirty minutes, when Harry picked up a singing bowl on the floor and struck it with its wooden stick. Instantly, a clear metallic musical sound spread out. Linda felt vibrating waves in the air, as if a dragonfly had touched the surface of a quiet lily pond.

Later they gathered around the table, refreshed, and holding large mugs of green tea.

"OK, my friends, what kind of spiritual pursuit are we seeking as a group?" Harry asked enthusiastically.

"A good question," said Andy, putting down his mug, "may I share my situation with you first?" Andy worked at a local nonprofit organization. His daily job included organizing meetings, writing speeches for his boss, and dealing with volunteers. "During the afternoons of most days, the noise in the office is unbearable, I feel I have lost the centre of my life, as if I were falling off a tightrope without a safe landing." Andy paused, looking at his new friends. "But it also seems to me that from time to time it's actually the noise that maintains the operation of our office." Andy had submitted a resignation to his boss once, but it was torn up, half-jokingly by his boss. "Most recently," Andy continued, "just in the last two weeks, I started to meditate during coffee breaks. I also invited a few volunteers to join me. After that, we definitely noticed a difference in productivity."

Andy concluded, saying he would like to explore meditation as a spiritual path towards inner peace. Harry nodded with empathy, while Linda listened attentively. She was taking notes, her right hand moved quickly on the surface of a notepad.

After sipping tea for a few minutes, Harry shared a totally different experience. The previous summer he and his wife, Fern, had spent two weeks meditating in the midst of the Rocky Mountains. He said he chose spots typically beyond the popular exploits of summer tourists. While retrieving his thoughts, his voice seemed to wander away, slowing down, and pausing here and there, as if he was revisiting the sceneries. He recalled that he sat in meditation daily for hours, rain or shine, like a tree or a piece of rock. When summer storms struck, he sat there just the same, rain splashing all over him. On sunny days, he meditated in the shades of large trees, listening to leaves quivering, bugs humming, and birds chirping on high branches. Sometimes he was not even aware of the secretive movements of small wild animals. Once a weasel was staring at him for more than ten minutes, another time a wild hare sat within a few feet. He recalled the mysterious mental state when he felt his own existence to be part of the mountains. In those moments, he said, he had experienced a genuine tranquility.

"Tranquility is happiness," Harry proclaimed softly, "the journey toward spirituality through tranquility is true happiness." Harry's eloquent reminiscences had Linda and Andy mesmerized. They got absorbed into his narrative. "Tranquility is happiness," Linda heard echoing in her mind, and she noted it down. She started to visualize mountain pines along rocky ridges under the blue sky.

"Are you intending to follow the ancient Taoists?" Linda asked. "They chose to dwell in remote mountains."

"You may say so. As you know, historically Taoists and Buddhists chose to meditate in remote natural settings," Harry replied. "Observing natural phenomena is important for spiritual transformation. And mystery happens during meditation." He paused, as if listening to his own thoughts. Then taking a deep breath, Harry stated, "I'm also struggling to figure out where I am heading in my art . . . "

The pen in Linda's hand halted on top of her notes. Staring at Harry, she knew it only too well—the trembling feelings of a middle-aged artist standing at a crossroad. She herself had been facing such a crossroad for some time now. These days she longed for new departures, but was not clear about her destination. Linda told her new friends that she felt all her departures had somehow returned her to the primary sources, herself and her life. Meeting them at the Aga Khan Museum, she assumed hopefully, could well be a new starting point for her spiritual and artistic journey.

At the end of their first meeting, seeing off the guests at the door, Harry said, "Lao Tzu says, true travellers don't plan their trips or know their destinations."

Arriving the following Tuesday afternoon for the group meditation, Linda noticed tiny blue flowers in the front lawn of Harry's house. "Spring is here!" Stepping into the hallway, "Guys—I have good news!" She was too excited to hold herself back. Her friends looked up and she asked them calmly, "Can we produce a stage presentation of Taoism in two months?"

"What is the event?" asked Harry, enthusiastically.

"Asian Heritage Month Festival, programmed under Asian Spiritual Wisdom."

"Great!" Andy said. "Got a venue yet?"

"Yes! The Aga Khan Museum! It has been scheduled for the last Sunday in May. It will be open to the public with free admission!"

Linda looked at her new friends expectantly.

"Shall we take up the challenge?" Harry asked calmly, raising his hand first. "Our first opportunity."

"Absolutely!" Andy also raised his hand, Linda joined in. It had suddenly dawned on them why they had met this spring and wanted to form a group. Now they could see clearly that they had a task awaiting.

Another week passed and more wild flowers, blue and white, covered the front lawn. The group of spiritual pursuers spent considerable time on the ancient text, *Tao Te Ching*, written about 500 BCE by the legendary Chinese wise man Lao Tzu.

"Is Taoism a religion?" Linda asked.

"Depends on the definition." Harry looked at Andy, who had a background in religious studies.

Andy picked up the thread. "There are two groups—theistic and non-theistic. The theistic group believes in a powerful Creator, whether God, Allah, or Brahma. They believe all existence, including human beings were created by the Creator."

"Buddhism and Taoism have no concept of an omnipotent Creator," said Harry, "are they not religions then?"

"No. Strictly speaking, Buddhists and Taoists are nonbelievers," confirmed Andy. "However, nontheistic faiths may also be based on spiritual practices."

"True," Harry nodded. "Buddhism shares a belief in the law of causality."

"What about following the laws of the natural world," asked Linda, "according to Lao Tzu?"

"Sure, the most important concept of Buddhism and Taoism is that Buddha and Lao Tzu were both mortal human beings," Andy clarified with an emphasis. "Their wisdom and knowledge came from practice."

With Linda nodding appreciatively, Andy concluded, "According to His Holiness the Dalai Lama, all sentient beings have Buddha-nature. Therefore, through practice, there is always a possibility for them to achieve Buddhahood. And Buddha is actually defined as an enlightened person."

"If we are persistent in our spiritual pursuits, we could be enlightened," Linda noted as they concluded their first group discussion.

Driving to Markham Village for group meditation gradually became an important routine for Linda. In the third week, she noticed massive dandelion blossoms along the highway. She couldn't miss their bright yellow colour. "How do dandelions display their overwhelming presence?" she thought aloud. As one of the most hated weeds, dandelions must have extremely resilient survival genes against mutation, so that they can continue to bloom bright yellow year after year. Entering the Village, Linda realized she could transform her inspiration from dandelions to an artistic approach.

"I think we can focus on a single verse from *Tao Te Ching* to maximize effective impact on the audience." She managed to deliver her suggestion without mentioning dandelions.

Much to her surprise, Harry responded agreeably, "I have been thinking the same thing."

"About the dandelions?" asked Linda curiously.

"What lions? About the image of water." Harry was not distracted by Linda, he continued with his own train of thought, "Verse 8 in *Tao Te Ching* summarizes the ultimate quality of water in one line 'Best to be like water.'"

"Best to be like water," echoed Andy, "Water is life, indispensable to all."

Linda agreed cheerfully, "Water makes up seventy-five percent of our body mass and weight."

Andy continued as if in a relay, "Water has three different physical forms, liquid, steam and ice."

Linda followed Andy with, "Water is in our blood and our brain. Water is always in our consciousness."

With a big smile, Harry asked, "What about water nourishing all lives without discrimination?"

"Oh, yes, that's most important!" Andy replied.

"Is water our choice then?" Harry raised his hand, Linda

followed. She then raised a question, "Now, how are we going to bring water into the performance? Since this will be a stage performance, the audience will expect entertainment."

"Entertainment?" Andy raised his eyebrows. "I thought we were going to share ancient Chinese wisdom."

"But nobody likes to be preached at. If we wrap ancient wisdom with entertainment, the audience will enjoy the performance and receive a dose of the wisdom," Linda explained.

"But I have no performing skills," apologized Andy, "unlike you two, I am not really an artist."

"Maybe it's time for you to become an artist—would you want to?" Harry asked seriously, "you need to let us know your answer before the end of the day, this is like an audition. You know we will give you adequate training, free of charge."

"We'll also share the artist fees with you after the performance," Linda added cheerfully.

"You mean we'll be paid as artists?" Andy's eyes shone in disbelief.

"You bet," said Linda. She switched the focus to the art forms involved in the performance. "We will have poetry, music, pantomime, theatrical acting, and so on."

"Don't forget Tai Chi movements, calligraphy, videography, and audience participation," Harry added. "It's going to be a contemporary, multimedia stage production!"

"Hey, Andy, I've got a new category for you," Linda said enthusiastically. "What about you being a meditative artist?"

"Meditative artist? Never heard of that before."

"Now you have," said Linda happily. "Through our performance, we will brand the new category of stage production and the artists involved."

"It sounds really exciting now. But, the idea of entertaining?" Harry uttered the word slowly as if thinking about its connotation and implication seriously for the first time. "OK, I think I can accept entertainment as a means to an end." He nodded at Linda. "Other means also include visual videos of lakes, rivers, mountains, and audio effects with the sound of wind and rain."

"What about live music? Another important means of entertainment," Andy suggested.

"Of course, live music, to arouse the acoustic senses of the audience."

They had arrived at unanimous agreement that it would be absolutely necessary to entertain the audience with an unusual stage presentation in order to introduce Taoism. They assigned the tasks accordingly, Linda would draft the poetic script to elaborate Lao Tzu's Verse 8. Harry would search his database for suitable video and audio clips. Andy would start practicing basic Tai Chi movements with Harry. Ultimately, the two men would be the performers on the stage, Linda would be the narrator, probably off stage with the musician. The team scheduled the creative process to begin in the coming week.

When Harry's wife, Fern, came home from work, Andy and Linda bid goodbye. The quiet residential neighbourhood streets were cloaked in the hazy pale shadows of streetlights.

"See the moon?" Andy asked Linda, as they were walking toward their parked cars.

"Moon?" Linda was surprised. "Where?" She looked up at the twilight evening sky.

Raising his right index finger, Andy pointed at the dark shadows of some remote trees. "Just slightly above the branches of the trees over there."

"Where? I still can't see it," Linda mumbled, disappointedly.

"Maybe my finger has blocked it."

"Blocking the moon?" Linda was confused. "With your finger? What kind of assumption is that?"

They laughed, waved goodbye, and drove away toward their homes.

While Linda was driving on the DVP the following Tuesday afternoon, she was stunned by the total change in the landscape along the highway. The overwhelming bright yellow dandelion blossoms had completely disappeared. Before her eyes was a huge wasteland with ghostly skeletons, the broken limbs of dandelion corpses, and the shadowy, aerial balls of their weightless flying seeds. Seeing the phenomenon, Linda realized that the limited time for dandelions to bloom their radiant yellow colour had passed, and they had entered another phase of life. Since joining the meditation group, she had become more sensitive to the seasonal changes in nature. And today, feeling like a budding spring dandelion, she was ready for their first creative workshop.

After a thirty-minute session of meditation, with a mug of green tea in her hand, Linda felt less anxious. Opening their laptops, Harry and Andy found Draft #1 that was sent by Linda before the meeting. Starting from that day, Linda explained, they would finalize all the stage directions with regards to every aspect of the performance. "Step by step, we will build the whole script and stage production together."

After further discussion of Lao Tzu's Verse 8, Harry stood up from the table, rubbing his hands, stretching his body. Gesturing to Andy to join him, Harry showed Andy some martial art positions, such as horse-riding, front-bow, back-bow, as well as how to walk on the stage. Then Harry picked up Andy's right hand and, face to face, he urged Andy, "Now push me off my feet."

Andy tried to push Harry, whose feet seemed rooted into the ground like a tree. Holding his breath, Andy pushed harder, Harry directed Andy's forward motion slightly to the side. Suddenly, Andy lost his balance and stepped out; he would have tripped over his own feet if Harry had not grabbed him in time.

Catching their breath, the men laughed loudly, and then they were ready to start again. Linda clapped her hands, "As your one and only audience member, I thank you for the entertainment."

"Entertainment?" The men threw back a rhetorical question.

So together they made a start, a rough start on the floor with some useful Tai Chi movements. Linda quickly edited the stage directions on her laptop with inspiration from the playful improvisation and tryouts of the men. By the end of the afternoon, they had gone through the first few pages of the manuscript. From the initial stage setup to Curtain Time to the end of Scene One, their multimedia stage production started to grow.

> *The name that can be named is not the eternal name,*
> *and the unnamable is the eternal,*
> *naming is for particular things.*

Linda repeated Lao Tzu's lines while driving home in the twilight. Traffic moved smoothly toward downtown. On the opposite side of the DVP, northbound traffic was nudging forward, bumper to bumper. Did people lose the centres of their lives, being stuck in a traffic jam every day? Linda recalled what Andy had once described as his daily job in the noisy office.

Time sped up on Linda's agenda when the group decided to meet twice a week. As a result, they had already completed the initial creative process. They had the script of a multimedia stage performance ready for rehearsal. Along the DVP, the dandelions had totally disappeared, having achieved the goals of their seasonal performance. Linda noticed that the tree leaves had changed from lemon green to dark green. In Markham Village, swinging gracefully in the soft spring breeze were yellow daffodils and colourful tulips, sending Linda a new message, "It's time to bloom!" as she entered Harry's house to start their first rehearsal.

Harry had sectioned off a part of the basement into a temporary rehearsal studio. It was surrounded by black curtains on three sides. Two spotlights pointed at the floor where Andy would be sitting in meditation at Curtain Time, according to the script. Harry had also set up a portable screen for video projection. A computer connected to the projector was plugged into a receptacle in the wall, ready to play video and audio clips. Before starting the rehearsal, Harry informed the team that Bruce, the musician, would join them in the afternoon.

They went through Scene One three times, with Linda quickly updating the draft. The insertion of video clips instantly produced amazing effects on the portable screen, such as heavy rain suddenly falling on a wild field. Its natural sound and visual impact overwhelmed the entire room, absorbing the attention of the actors. Harry's original video footages were shot in Asia and South and North America, where he had practiced meditation.

In the afternoon, Bruce arrived with two amplifiers, boxes of connecting devices, and his electric guitar. With live music, the group embarked on another exciting new phase of the rehearsal. A recurrent melody which Linda named, *Blue Sky, White Clouds*, flew out of the guitar strings, filling up the entire house. Linda quickly updated stage directions to conform with the music.

Near the end of the day, when the team came upstairs for tea, Fern had come home from work. Andy proposed that they should invite family members and friends to watch their next rehearsal. Though it was a bit too early, everybody agreed.

Sunday afternoon, driving north on the DVP, Linda felt as if she were on a different highway. Most drivers actually followed the speed limit, instead of passing and crossing multiple lanes. The team was scheduled to meet at three pm, and the rehearsal for family members and friends was scheduled for five pm, followed by feedback with tea and snacks.

"I have a surprise for all of you," said Andy when the group had gathered in Harry's basement. "I have invited a family friend, who is a producer of public concerts in Hong Kong and China. He will arrive at four to watch our rehearsal and give us his professional advice."

"Wow, that's a surprise!" Linda responded hesitatingly. "Honestly, we're not ready yet."

"I am still trying different chords," said Bruce, while tuning his guitar.

"Let's hope he will be able to help us at this stage," said Harry.

At four o'clock sharp, the Hong Kong producer arrived. "I have to leave exactly at four-thirty," said Mr Wong, when Andy welcomed him down to the basement.

> *The name that can be named is not the eternal name,*
> *and the unnamable is the eternal,*
> *naming is for particular things.*

Linda started the rehearsal. With the producer as the first audience, the team actually went through the entire script without stopping. Reaching the end, they looked at the clock on the wall, "Twenty-two minutes, perfect!"

Producer Wong was taking notes during the rehearsal. Checking his watch, he commented, "Overall you are not ready to perform yet. Your familiarity and confidence are at only fifty percent," he said plainly. The team members nodded their agreement. "Since you still have a week before the show, you would improve rapidly if I were your producer." He looked at Andy.

"Sorry we have no funding for this project," Andy apologized. "We can't afford to pay you as our producer." The team was also embarrassed, making eye contact with each other.

"If that's the situation," responded Mr Wong softly. A smile was fading from his face. "I still want to help you. Just put my name as the producer in the program, that'd be OK."

Harry approved happily. "It would be a great honour to have you as our producer! And free of charge, thank you very much! We agree!" The decision was made and Producer Wong left the house. "See you all at the Aga Khan Museum at ten am next Sunday!"

"What does a producer do for a small stage production like ours?" Linda asked her teammates.

"For movies," Harry elaborated, "I understand the producer pays for all the costs."

"But for a small stage performance like ours," argued Bruce, "there is no need for a producer. There should be a director for drama, for an elaborate symphony orchestra, a conductor."

"Well, the point is we are not paying him. We've got the best bargain," Harry concluded.

"That's true. I made it clear that we can't afford to hire him," said Andy. "Mr Wong handles public concerts for thousands of people in Hong Kong and China."

"Wow, so we are lucky to have him for free," remarked Bruce reluctantly. "And hopefully, his professional experience will help us." The team agreed.

The last Sunday of May finally arrived. *Blue Sky, White Clouds*, the melody was floating in the air. Orange, blue, and yellow pansies flashing their pretty faces in the early summer breeze, the air smelt of fresh soil and sprouting shoots. Soft sunshine cast moving shadows on the sidewalks, as if chasing white clouds in the sky.

The team gathered in the lobby of the Aga Khan Museum at ten o'clock sharp. Some family members, friends, supporters, and volunteers had also arrived. The team was anxious to set up the stage and test the equipment, especially the lighting. They were anxious to have an on-site rehearsal before the scheduled show time at one pm.

Linda found the lighting specialist assigned by the Museum to work with her team. She gave the technician a copy of the script, on which all the lighting instructions were highlighted with a light blue marker. She also explained to the technician that there would be two occasions for audience participation, during which floor lights should be turned on for the audience to see each other. When Linda was about to ask the technician for an on-site rehearsal as soon as possible, Mr Wong came into the control room on the second floor.

"You should not be here!" Mr Wong said to Linda in an authoritative voice. "I'm the producer, I will work with the technician." Linda was shocked. Mr Wong actually pushed her towards the door. Once she was out, he stepped into the cluttered small space.

Linda came down to the audience floor to greet her friends, who had been supporters of the annual Asian Heritage Month Festival for years. She saw her friend Ping walk into the auditorium and toward her. Linda had invited Ping to be the photographer of the day.

"Why are you still here?" A harsh voice struck Linda's back like a slingshot. She didn't know if the voice was addressing her or someone else. She instinctively resented the tone of the voice. Nobody had the right to shout at her. Turning around, Linda was facing Mr Wong again, the self-invited producer of their performance.

"Excuse me, Mr Wong, what did you say?" Linda tried to sound normal.

"I asked why you are still here," Mr Wong didn't hesitate to repeat.

"I am here to talk to the photographer, I have invited her to take photos of the performance."

"You are a performer today. You should behave like a star, and I will treat you like a star. Right now, you should be resting in Dressing Room 2 until I call you."

Linda burst out laughing, "Sure, but not before I dealt with the lighting technician until you came to push me out. Now I just need to talk to the photographer about the angles, so she can reserve a few seats. In fact, there is an urgent need that could actually have your executive attention." Linda said slowly and respectfully, "The team desperately needs an on-site rehearsal, or at least, a walk through the scenes on the new stage. Would you please arrange it with the lighting technician as soon as possible?"

Mr Wong replied, "Please leave the stage management to me. And now you should go to Dressing Room 2 immediately!"

At this point, the guest photographer gestured at Linda by waving her hand. "Go, Linda, get some rest before the show."

Suddenly, Linda had lost the concept of what she was doing; as Andy said once, she was falling off the tightrope without a safe landing. She and her teammates had been patiently training for two months. They had been evaluating each movement in order to walk across the stage successfully. Today they were here to inspire and entertain the audience with a different kind of stage production. This stranger, who came to their rehearsal once for thirty minutes, and invited himself to be their producer, now was trying to deprive her of her duty to take care of her responsibilities. "Behave like a star?" Linda laughed silently, a sour taste in her mouth. "What a cliché! A stereotypical Hollywood cliché! And totally irrelevant." Her team had started the project without any funding; it would end without being noticed by any media. The performance had been created solely through their joint labour of love. The fancy word, stardom, had never crossed their minds during the entire process.

With her hand against the wall of the dark passage to the

backstage, Linda paused for a long moment to take a few deep breaths. She recalled the initial meeting of the team at this museum. Right beside the information desk, the three of them had talked for an hour without moving their feet. She also remembered Harry's monologue about his artistic career being at a crossroads, looking for a contemporary art form to challenge mediocrity and constraints to creativity. This conception of multimedia stage performance had, miraculously, resulted from their joint spiritual journey. They wanted to share it with the public. Their performance would hopefully attract five hundred Canadians of different backgrounds to the Aga Khan Museum. For the majority of them, it would be their first time to visit the Islamic Museum. All this was probably unheard-of by Mr Wong and the stars he dealt with.

When Linda found Dressing Room 1, Harry, Bruce, and Andy were all there, as were several student volunteers. Realizing that they must be hungry, she brought out bags of food that she and others had purchased and prepared the night before. "Lunch time, everyone!" Suddenly, she felt grateful that she could take care of the needs of the team and the volunteers. As a group of spiritual pursuers, their team had never strictly divided areas of service other than collaboration and mutual support. She hoped they would never again allow an aggressive, disrespectful intruder to destroy the purpose and the process of their spiritual and artistic journey.

"Are we having an on-site rehearsal?" Harry asked Linda earnestly.

She shook her head, "I don't know, it's up to Mr Producer."

Harry must know how she felt.

"It's twelve-fifteen pm now, let's meditate for thirty minutes as usual." He called Andy and Bruce. They went next door for a moment of tranquility.

At 12:50 pm, Mr Wong came to Dressing Room 1. "I am glad you are all here," he said. "It's time to wait in the wings." The team stood up. Andy was dressed completely in whites, including his socks and shoes, to symbolize *yang* of the Tai Chi icon; Harry, on the other hand, was dressed completely in black as *yin* of the Tai Chi icon. Linda wore a black outfit with a white shirt inside, revealing a white edge under the black jacket; Bruce was in a white sweatshirt with black pants.

Despite the stress and anxiety from the long period of waiting, the team didn't show it on their faces. However, without an on-site rehearsal, or even a walk-through on the stage, uncertainty was apparent in all their eyes. Mr Producer took the team to the large screen behind the stage. They saw a full house! On the stage, the Artistic Director of the museum was giving his welcome speech to the audience.

"Do your best, if anything goes wrong, just carry on!" Mr Producer stuck out his hand and was joined by the hands of the performers. "Let's go!" They felt blood rushing through their veins. It was time to show their best!

Once she was standing behind the podium, Linda started immediately to search for the control buttons for the slides and video, as she had been previously instructed by the producer. But there were none on all four sides of the podium. Time was ticking away loudly in her head. The audience members were all staring at the stage, expecting her to start. Cold sweat was running down her spine; she realized that the arrangements had been changed, but she had not been updated. As a last-minute solution, she raised her left index finger just slightly above her head, hoping this gesture would be received as her signal for the lighting technician to start the show.

It worked. Lao Tzu's picture appeared on the wall of the back stage, taking the audience's attention immediately away from the podium. Relieved, Linda delivered a brief introduction about Lao Tzu and *Tao Te Ching*. When she raised her left index finger again, the lighting technician changed the screen smoothly to the next slide.

Linda started to relax behind the podium. She watched her team unroll the rich content of their creation from ancient to contemporary culture, including philosophical and environmental perspectives, as well as individual and collective values. The audience members were far from being overwhelmed by unfamiliar materials; instead, they were entertained by the multiple art forms, including poetry, music, martial art, and beautiful video clips of natural scenes. Harry and Andy, the two main performers, moved around the stage. At some point, audience members were invited to participate in standing meditation on the floor. Harry also walked down from the stage to play Tai Chi pushing hands with a few volunteer audience members, both men and women. With a well-measured and alternated rhythm of motion and tranquility on and off the stage, Lao Tzu's wisdom, "Best to be like water," had been shared by the audience of five hundred men and women from different backgrounds.

Throughout the thirty-minute performance, the lighting technician made a couple of mistakes, jamming two slides into one, and throwing the narrator and performers into disorder. However, the two performers quickly recovered and continued with the performance. They did it seamlessly and the audience didn't notice anything abnormal.

When one more lighting mistake happened near the end of the performance, Linda decided to skip a couple of lines. She jumped to the ending scene by inviting some volunteers from the audience to come to the stage for a group Tai Chi with the performers. In just a few minutes, the stage became crowded, and the rest of the audience lined up on the floor to join the practice. The production ended with Harry leading five hundred people doing Tai Chi movements on and off the stage. With "Best to Be Like Water" being projected onto the backstage wall, the performance reached a climax of spiritual togetherness.

When Linda was back on the DVP again, driving toward Markham Village, it was already mid-summer. An entire month had passed since the team successfully performed on the stage of the Aga Khan Museum. Along the north-south throughway, dense vegetation had already merged into a uniform colour of dark green. In Harry's neighbourhood, flowers were blooming vibrantly in front of all the houses, roses of different colours, yellow and orange chrysanthemums, and hydrangea with large white, blue, or pink flowers. Linda fitted right in with her fashionable pink T-shirt and a white-laced cotton skirt. "Summer is the season of productivity in nature, what should we do next?" she asked herself, entering the lobby of Harry's house.

With time passing, the teammates had forgotten some details of their latest public performance. They had also distanced themselves from the intrusive Mr Producer. But they vividly remembered the overwhelming enthusiasm of the audience, who had expressed serious interest in their unique stage performance of the ancient wisdom of Taoism.

"After the show, some audience members asked me if we teach meditation," Andy recalled.

"A couple told me they enjoyed the performance very much, because it was very different," Harry recalled. "They asked me if we have other shows."

"Seriously, we have fans now," said Linda excitedly. "My daughter has added standing meditation to her daily athletic training program after participating in our show. An artist friend called to tell me she bought a copy of *Tao Te Ching* after our performance."

Sharing feedback from the audience gratified them. As they sat around the table, eating summer berries, the fruits tasted riper and more delicious.

"What's our next step?" Linda inquired.

"We have planted seeds," Harry was retrieving his thoughts slowly. "Seeds are destined to sprout, some have a chance to root and become part of the forest in the future." Andy and Linda listened attentively, hopeful to share their spiritual practice and artistic creativity with the public. Harry finished his reflection, "It's time for us to return to primary sources and meditation."

"I agree," echoed Andy immediately. "We have been too busy to focus on our own inner peace for quite some time. It's time for us to return to the path." Upon this, a deep respect and admiration for her teammates arose in Linda. She remembered Lao Tzu's saying that return is the movement of the Tao. Both her teammates had been on the spiritual path for a much longer time.

They decided to go for a thirty-minute walking meditation behind Harry's house. They had spoken about it for quite some time. They stepped out through the sliding door of the kitchen into cool fresh air and soft sunshine.

What a delightful renewal, just being in the woods! Stretching out their arms freely like tree branches, they could hear each other inhaling and exhaling, loudly and deeply. They wandered around, meditating naturally along the winding path for almost an hour before returning to the house.

Fern was already home, washing vegetables and preparing dinner. "I had no idea where you guys were. You haven't even had your afternoon tea." She brought the terracotta mugs of green tea to the table. Linda and Andy realized it was nearly time for them to end the afternoon meeting, but they sat down anyway for the late afternoon tea. To their surprise, Harry didn't seem to notice the passing time. While sipping his tea, Harry started an unexpected new topic. He said that after sharing a walking meditation with his teammates, he felt strongly about sharing some particulars of his personal spiritual practices.

Harry and Fern came to Canada from Hong Kong before their homeland was officially returned to China in 1997, having been a British colony for ninety-nine years. Back in Hong Kong, Harry was a successful comic artist for newspapers and magazines. Upon landing in Canada, he didn't know what he could do other than to persist stubbornly with his firm belief that he would not give up his career as a professional artist. Throughout the years, he struggled as a new immigrant and as an artist, until finally he established his private art school and made a decent living. More important than paying bills, he has branded contemporary abstract ink painting and Tai Chi calligraphy into mainstream Canadian art scenes.

Harry said his artistic pursuits had always been part of his spiritual journey. Fern, standing at the stove, turned around to listen to her husband. Harry said he was willing to share his secrets with his friends. "I have been getting up at four am every morning to meditate."

"For thirty years, since we came to Canada," Fern confirmed.

"However, although four am meditation is my regular practice, I also have an emergency practice when I run into a personal or career crisis."

"What's that?" asked Fern curiously. Linda and Andy laughed.

"I get up at midnight to meditate all night while the world is soundly asleep."

Harry elaborated that since moonlight reaches the earth in one minute, he actually asked the moon to be the witness to his karmic struggle. "I would swear to the moon that I needed to be an artist in order to be myself." He would sit in the moonlight throughout the night, talking to the moon, observing the moon on its path, and from time to time, he would feel a special ray of hope directly from the moon. By dawn, when *yin* and *yang* energy reached a new equilibrium in the universe for a new day, he had achieved his inner peace. "'Be one with the universe,' as Lao Tzu said. I managed to set myself free from my crisis." A serene expression appeared on Harry's face, his eyes were looking somewhere that Linda couldn't reach.

Fern asked the two artists to stay for a simple family dinner. Andy apologized, saying that his wife had just called, he had to leave. Linda was delighted to accept the invitation with a strong lingering intention to preserve this precious moment. Harry's personal spiritual relationship with the moon had touched her in a way she couldn't quite identify yet.

Fern set the table with three pairs of chopsticks before bringing over the food from the kitchen counter. Once seated at the table, Harry asked Fern if she wanted to say her usual invocation. "Sure," Fern bent her head slightly forward to thank God for bringing talented artist friends into their house. She also thanked God for helping the team successfully deliver the performance a month ago. Finally, she thanked God for the nutritious food on the table to be shared with their guest tonight. "Amen," Fern ended her prayer. Harry and Linda followed with their "Amen."

"Just to let you know, Fern is a Christian," Harry clarified. "As a married couple, we respect each other's spirituality." Sometimes, Harry said, he would go to church with Fern on Sundays.

Later that night, driving home on the DVP, Linda was overwhelmed by the bright moonlight, not only lighting up the entire landscape along the highway, but also pouring into her car as if from a fountain of silver light beams. She realized her own spiritual journey was also being witnessed by the moon. Her eyes were suddenly filled up, tears rolling down her cheeks. She had experienced an ultrasensitive moment of inner peace.

In June, peonies were blooming with their luxurious colours in front of the many prosperous large properties in Markham Village. Linda guessed that most of these property owners were likely Chinese, because peonies were culturally regarded as the flowers of wealth and prosperity which had long become a motif in traditional Chinese brush paintings. In Fern's garden, besides peonies, there were also many annuals and perennials growing wild with multiple colourful blossoms. Harry had built a rock garden at the back of the house in addition to the large deck. There were also found objects in the rock garden, pieces of driftwood, the abandoned wheel of an old farm vehicle, and rusty iron window frames. Some irregular white granite pieces formed a spiritual path from under the deck to the woods as a physical *Feng Shui* connection.

For their midsummer meeting, the group decided to deal with an important agenda. They wanted to brand a collective name before taking up any new projects. Linda had raised the question before, but now was a better time to brainstorm their vision for the future.

Sitting comfortably on the deck, Harry felt it natural to reinstate his perspective of the future. "You've known me now for some time and I am not going to change my path of thirty years. Regarding the name for our group, what about Moon Pointing Productions, the name that Andy mentioned some time ago?"

Andy reached out to his document folder, from which he took a couple of business cards for Harry and Linda to see. It was a fold-up card, so it could stand up on its own like a roof. The background of the card was navy blue, with a waxing crescent moon and the company name printed in bright yellow. Andy's name as Creative Director with contact information was printed in white.

"A nice design!" exclaimed Linda.

"Very nice, indeed, Andy!" said Harry. "Congratulations!"

Harry and Linda could see that their teammate had been serious about meditation for a long time, and so he had already registered a business name for the practice. "So, Andy," asked Harry, "what kind of products and programs have you and your company produced? Do you have any partners?"

"I registered the company name a few years ago," said Andy, "but I haven't developed any programs yet. At this stage, it's a sole ownership." He smiled apologetically.

"I see—" responded Harry thoughtfully. "As you know, I really like the name."

"I do too," Linda echoed, "especially because 'productions' is the anchor of the business."

"Thank you." Andy smiled happily at this affirmation. Sipping tea for a few minutes, they pondered the subject.

After a pause, Harry asked two direct questions to further clarify his intent. "Andy, can we join Moon Pointing Productions as your partners? Or can we work under your incorporation as a subgroup?"

"I don't see why we can't work under the name Moon Pointing Productions," Andy said.

"That's great," answered Harry immediately. "I will design another logo. We will brand the company as a unique multimedia performance troupe."

Another long pause, the team sipped tea, thinking in silence.

Should there be an affirming vote and signing of an agreement? Or, at least, circulating a memorandum among them confirming the agreement? Linda thought about this for a while; any serious business company would want to document an important verbal agreement such as this one. While they continued to sip tea, Linda asked herself, without a binding agreement, how long could they keep their shared vision intact?

The meeting moved on to formal matters. The team decided to assign key roles among themselves. Andy, as the original founder, should be the president of the corporation, Harry the artistic director, and Linda the business manager. So theoretically, though only verbally, the three of them were now the elected officers of Moon Pointing Productions Inc. They also passed a motion with unanimous agreement that the three of them would be the core partners of the business; a triangle would always be the best structure for strength and stability. Other artists would be hired for future performances and paid for the occasion.

"Let's stick to multimedia inter-art stage performances," said Harry. "We will brand the new contemporary genre and style on the stage."

"After we build up a portfolio of a few performances, we can tour Vancouver, Calgary, and Montreal for the annual Asian Heritage Month Festival in May," suggested Andy.

Near the end of the meeting, Linda said, "Enjoy the midsummer and dream creatively."

"Linda, what a poetic way to end our meeting!" They were heading to the front door, Harry behind his teammates. "By the way, I will be travelling to Asia for a month in August. I plan to visit some old temples. I will meditate on our future."

"Meditate on our future? Great idea, I will do the same in my parents' cottage," added Andy, putting on his outdoor leather sandals. Linda said she would practice walking meditation by Lake Ontario.

Standing by her parked car, Linda saw on the western horizon an overwhelming crimson sunset, forecasting another bright sunny day to come. She looked for the moon in the clear cloudless sky, but not even a faint outline was detectable. Nevertheless, she knew, the moon was there, a waxing crescent at this hour, not easily perceivable by human eyes. As the earth rotated through the night, there would eventually be a bright moon in the sky. Andy was waving at her from his driver's seat with the window down, Linda waved back.

In late September, leaves started to change colour. Along the DVP, brilliant sugar maples displayed their scarlet red colour toward the blue sky. Birch and poplar leaves were turning bright yellow, a few swirling away from the branches and spinning down to the ground. Sumac bushes presented the most meaningful colour for Linda, a variation of enriched red between pink and burgundy. Autumn is nature's annual celebration after its peak growth in the summer. Within a month and a half, nature's grandiose annual show would come to an end after its splendid performance, then it would bow to the audience with its massive curtains of falling leaves. Driving on the DVP in the rich autumn colours brought Linda an indescribable joy, an intuitive sense of fulfillment and worthiness.

Andy joined Linda as she was admiring the flowers in the front garden of Harry's house.

"Fern definitely has a green thumb," Linda commented.

"You look like you've got exciting news," said Andy, speculating.

"What? Are you a fortune teller today?"

"I can tell from the sunshine on your face," said Andy with a smile.

"Oh, that's my seasonal colour like a sugar maple," said Linda happily.

"OK, Sugar Maple!" They walked into the house together. "Harry, Linda's got good news!"

Harry's voice came from an inside room. "Shall we meditate first before hearing the news?"

"Of course."

On the floor, as usual, they sat in a triangle to draw energy from each other. Andy set his phone for thirty minutes. Harry struck the singing bowl with the wooden stick. Pure metallic sound spread out like a breeze, touching their faces, hair, lips, and eardrums with its vibrations. Linda could feel the inhaling and exhaling of her fellow meditators. She followed the same rhythm, deep and slow, neither rushed nor hushed, her mind concentrated on an inner space through her breathing. At the top of her mind, there were blue sky and white clouds. She stayed there peacefully within its tranquility for as long as she could, until the phone's musical bell gently brought their mental focus back to reality.

Sitting at the table with fresh green tea, the men waited for Linda's news. Linda said quietly that she had potential good news for next spring and she also had a list of questions accumulated during the summer break. "Which part do you want to hear first?"

Andy looked at Harry, and said, "Next spring is still far away, let's hear the questions first, right Harry?"

"Sure," Harry gestured for Linda to begin.

"OK, the first question for Andy, when you registered Moon Pointing Productions as a business enterprise, what was the original inspiration and what were the products you had in mind? Do you still remember?"

"Oh, yes, I do remember what triggered me to register the business name," answered Andy without giving it a second thought. "To tell you the truth, I was seriously thinking about opening a specialty store to market meditation cushions." He paused to look at his teammates, "In those days, I dreamt of seeing everyone going to work, carrying a meditation cushion on their back."

"Are you serious?" Linda couldn't help but burst out laughing. With her eyes wide open, she stared at Andy, "So did you open the specialty store?"

"No, shortly after I registered the company, I found out the cost of making those cushions was too expensive to move ahead as a starting product. Plus, I wasn't even sure there would be enough customers." Andy laughed reflectively. "It is definitely important to introduce more people to meditation first."

"By the way, I am not laughing at your initial business idea,"

Linda apologized. "In fact, it's a creative idea." She continued, "The British Parliament has recently introduced meditation as a daily practice for its members' health and wellness. It has been reported that the practice has already improved the mindfulness and attentiveness of the members."

"That's amazing!" Harry said. "Andy, your chance will be coming in ten years to run a wholesale business selling meditation cushions!" They all laughed together this time. Harry continued, "Can you tell us what kind of business products that you dream about now?"

"I want to find out the ultimate in the midst of daily life," said Andy.

"That's quite abstract, whose daily life, yours or others'?"

"Both. I wish to bring more people into tranquility through meditation. To me, each stage of tranquility is reaching the moon." Andy looked serious and thoughtful.

"Actually, I have a question about this," Linda jumped in to ask her next question. "During meditation, we concentrate on breathing, trying to stop wandering thoughts, in order to enter a state of tranquility. Is tranquility the final goal of meditation?"

"Tranquility is a nonreactive state," Andy explained. "When you stop doing things, you halt all movement and action, not even trying to figure out about tranquility."

Linda scratched her head. "Would you compare reaching tranquility with stopping at a traffic light at an intersection? Nothing happens for a few minutes. Then traffic resumes as before."

"What do you think traffic lights do to the drivers and pedestrians?"

Linda knew traffic lights too well to need a second thought. "The minutes of nonreactive state could have prevented some drivers from rushing into unwanted situations. But this logic seems to indicate an assumption that rushing into a solution may be inadequate or even dangerous." Linda felt as if she was arguing with Andy.

"I think so," Andy agreed, "meditation helps people relax mental stress and tension. The truth is that we don't have to offer solutions on the spot," Andy said with emphasis, "but that's only partially why we meditate."

"I think meditation may encourage procrastination or indecisiveness," Linda continued, following her own train of thought.

"Maybe, and maybe not," Andy shrugged his shoulders.

"Mindfulness or full awareness through meditation opens doors to inner peace or transformation," Harry added his perspective. "The realm is in meditation, it's a mysterious process."

"Harry, you've just introduced a new concept," Linda was alert.

"Have I?" Harry looked at his teammates, a bit surprised. "What did I say?"

"You said 'the realm is in meditation,'" Linda said, repeating Harry's words. "What do you mean by that?"

"Oh, realm, it refers to all potentials, obtainable and unobtainable, expected and unexpected during meditation," Harry replied. "But nobody can ever predict when and how the transformation will take place, or if it will even occur."

"One last question for the afternoon," announced Linda. "Why do you think others need you to point at the moon for them? The pointing business may backfire with an illusion that the pointer is superior, or worse, a savior."

"Oh, no, it shouldn't be," remarked Andy. "Spiritual pursuit is a personal choice. Inner peace is a personal path toward true freedom. The realm exists in meditation, as people focus on different areas of life. You can have a group of people meditate together, but no meditator can deliver inner peace into another person's consciousness. Every person's pursuit is contingent on his or her own experience."

They were carried away by their discussion until Fern came back from work. Linda and Andy bid goodbye to Harry. They didn't have time to talk about the potential good news until their next meeting.

The following Tuesday afternoon, when they finally sat around the table, sipping tea, the men smiled at Linda, "What's the potential good news for next spring, Linda? You have kept us waiting for two weeks."

"You guys have demonstrated unbelievable focus, some kind of mental power to distance yourselves from potential temptation," Linda said. Now that she was expected to deliver the news, her voice remained calm in order not to arouse a strong reaction from her teammates.

As the business manager of Moon Pointing Productions, Linda said, she had tentatively accepted an invitation from a national academic organization. The organization expressed an interest in having their team deliver a multimedia performance at its annual conference early next May.

"Not bad!" Andy exclaimed, looking around the table. "We must have impressed some members of the organization with our performance at the Aga Khan Museum."

"I'm sure we did. This is the first invitation for our team to perform before a designated audience," Harry said thoughtfully. "Obviously, we can't use the same script as the one for a general public audience of five hundred people."

"That's right," Linda agreed.

"So what kind of audience will we be performing for?" Andy asked.

"This time, the audience will be a small group of professors," Linda explained, "each one of them a social-cultural-literary critic. And they have asked us to entertain them during their annual academic conference, isn't that incredible?"

"Absolutely! But how do we entertain them?"

They sipped green tea, pondering over the subject.

Before long, Harry changed the subject. "I'm not sure if I have shared with you one of my other peculiarities—" He looked at his teammates with a grin.

"How many more peculiarities do you have, Harry?" Linda asked half-jokingly. It was two years since they first met. They had shared many meditations and discussions and knew each other almost like siblings.

"Oh, yes, I have others," Harry admitted, "but this peculiarity is more serious." He looked at Andy and then Linda before he continued, "I have a living artist's principle. It governs all the activities of my life as an artist." He paused for a minute. "Whatever I do, I do not repeat."

Andy and Linda were speechless. It took Linda more than a couple of minutes before she could respond, "Lao Tzu says return is the movement of the Tao."

"I understand," agreed Harry, "but return doesn't mean repeat." He then clarified what he meant by not repeating. "Especially for public performances, I would refuse to present the same work twice." Hearing this, Andy and Linda immediately looked at each other, realizing that they could never become a performance troupe.

"Why did you adopt such a restriction?" Andy's voice was loud and emotional.

"I'll tell you why. Again, it relates to my spiritual pursuit." Before Harry went on to explain, his teammates said they needed a two-minute break to add hot water to their tea mugs, and perhaps use the washroom.

When they returned to the table, expecting a long story, Harry delivered the philosophical and spiritual ground of his living artist's principle in only four words, "Rebirth is an illusion."

"What?" Linda felt lightheaded. In her mind's eye, she saw the beautiful mythical bird arising from its own ashes and spreading its wings toward the blue sky. Rebirth had been indispensable for her own imagination as well as for the female characters in her stories. It gave them the courage to depart from grim circumstances and move toward a new beginning.

Now Harry was elaborating on his artist's principle. "Rebirth is an illusion because it is a craving just like all other desires." Andy was nodding at Harry, Linda could tell that rebirth didn't mean the same to Andy and Harry as it did to her. Rebirth had been an ancient human vision regarding death and beyond. It followed the reproductive law in the natural world. Linda's train of thought was interrupted by Andy's voice this time, "Rebirth addresses a deep fear in human consciousness, because death is inevitable."

Linda agreed with Andy, but simultaneously she wanted to put out a serious experiential argument. "Human society needs courage to survive hardship and only hope can sustain that courage. Therefore, the concepts of rebirth and reincarnation were introduced—to give hope beyond human suffering in Buddhism."

"But don't you care if a strong craving was attached to rebirth?" Harry asked Linda.

"No, not for the reasons I have felt strongly about," answered Linda firmly. She then shared with her teammates the daily self-affirmation that His Holiness the Dalai Lama had been repeating for decades:

> *Illusions still exist,*
> *reincarnation not completed,*
> *willing to remain in the world,*
> *to help others end sufferings.*

"Wow, His Holiness clearly points out that reincarnation is related to illusion. Nevertheless, in order to take care of the community, he still chose rebirth." Harry let out a deep sigh, picking up his tea mug. Linda heard him swallowing instead of sipping the liquid. After a long pause, Harry uttered one word, "Compassion."

Linda and Andy nodded their agreement.

When Harry resumed, he said firmly, "I don't disagree with the concept of rebirth as a natural, reasonable, foundational concept from its agricultural roots. But for me, a contemporary artist, I've made great efforts to reject rebirth in my personal life as well as my artistic practice."

"What do you mean by rejecting rebirth?" Linda asked seriously.

"First of all, in my personal life, I refused to have children," answered Harry. "Fern and I had agreed many years ago that we would not produce children, so we wouldn't have our imperfections repeated in them."

"Are you serious, Harry?" Linda burst out emotionally. "Did Fern become a kindergarten teacher, because she didn't have her own children?"

"Precisely," Harry confirmed. "You know we both enjoy teaching children and youth."

Andy and Linda looked at each other. They picked up their mugs, slowly and silently sipped their tea. They continued to ponder on what Harry had shared with them.

Driving home in the early evening, Linda couldn't disengage herself from the subject of the afternoon's discussion. She realized that Harry, in fact, was a strong believer in reincarnation. Therefore, he had been determined to challenge his fate. According to him, his living artist's principle had been his spiritual practice to avoid reincarnation. But wasn't his concept of final freedom just another illusion or craving?

Moving along with the early evening traffic, Linda felt that she was floating downstream on top of a peaceful river. She couldn't resist its momentum. Like a drop of water, her existence could only be ratified in a stream, a river, a lake, or an ocean. She remembered another profound statement by His Holiness the Dalai Lama regarding the interdependence between an individual's physical and spiritual wellness and humanity. If you still care about the community, his Holiness said, you need to stay involved. Reincarnation, theoretically and spiritually, remains the only path.

After Halloween, large brown paper bags filled with fallen leaves were lined up along Toronto's residential neighbourhood streets. Temperatures started to drop. The Canadian winter could easily last for half a year. From December to April Canadians strategically chose to stay indoors rather than drive miles to knock on a friend's door.

During their last meeting in late autumn, the group of spiritual pursuers decided to take a seasonal break to avoid unnecessary winter driving under unpredictable weather and road conditions. During the long break, each person would continue to meditate at home on how to entertain the academics with a multimedia stage production next spring. They unanimously agreed not to repeat any episode from their previous performance, in accordance with Harry's living artist's principle. And they happily bid goodbye to each other with, "Merry Christmas! Happy New Year! Happy Chinese New Year! See you next spring!"

Months passed, with snow storms, icy rain, and slippery driving conditions. Finally, after all the winter holidays had come and gone, Linda was back on the DVP driving toward Markham Village, overjoyed to see bright yellow dandelion blossoms by the millions again. This was the second year since meeting Harry and Andy. They had come a long way as a group of spiritual pursuers and creative artists. For the new spring season, they had a special audience to entertain. She felt a stirring excitement. As if the soil had embraced the seeds of summer blooms, the team had an immediate seasonal task awaiting.

After their meditation, the group returned to the table for discussion. Over tea they started to unleash creative ideas and suggestions, shedding new light on the potential of their next performance.

"First of all, I don't think our performance needs to be based on one unified theme or subject, what do you think?" Harry started the discussion.

"Mm, a good approach," echoed Linda and Andy. Finally, the team chose the art form of collage. Each performer had a chance to present a solo episode in addition to various supporting roles in the overall performance. They named their new performance, "Awakening the Land Within Us."

"Wow, this could be our most experimental work!" Harry exclaimed loudly.

The university lounge offered the ideal layout and space for a small audience of fifty, who could see the performance from any angle in the room. The stage was on ground level and only ten feet in front of the seats.

Linda delivered a monologue in the beginning of Scene Two: Personal Struggles. She was strolling slowly in front of the seats, hoping her close presence would arouse self-awareness and self-reflection in the audience. While she was speaking to the audience in the two front rows, she noticed a young woman nodding in agreement with her, as she addressed the tainted nature of words:

> words can be violent weapons
> as sticks and stones can kill
> or to stifle your voice
> making a trembling silence

Linda sighted an old gentleman sitting in the front row. She stood in front of him, as if they were having a face-to-face conversation. He intuitively shifted his sitting position, before staring at her for the next stanza:

> *words frame us, words trapping us*
> *we wrestle with them like warriors, or*
> *indulge ourselves with their magic power,*
> *day in day out, like opioid drug addicts*

The expression of the old gentleman remained a blank page, without a twitch of emotion, as if his facial muscles had been frozen by multiple Botox injections. But how could he not be amused or touched by Linda's self-mockery? She didn't separate herself from the audience. Once upon a time, she was their colleague. Today she was here to challenge the profession.

The last stanza was dedicated to Linda's two sisters, Ming and Yun, and other professional women who had died of ovarian cancer at a prime age. Linda expressed her compassion for their sufferings, their decades spent in overwork, their physical exhaustion, the little time they had for their own health:

> *in the battlefields of your profession, you were*
> *the foot soldiers, and the fallen heroes*
> *across the pages, row on row*
> *the poppies blow*

Following Linda's poems, Andy performed a pantomime of chasing illusions while Harry produced illusive shadows with a portable projector in his hands. The shadows moved from the floor to the walls, which enclosed the audience in an invisible circle, illustrating human desire to achieve too many goals in life. Andy mock-collapsed in front of the audience.

Live music and video clips introduced the audience to Scene

Three, in which Harry performed brush painting on three dif-
ferent-sized canvases. The last one was the largest, 5 by 5 feet in
size. Andy was sitting on the floor holding up the canvas frame
for Harry to work on. An image of the Canadian prairie was projected onto the drop-down back stage screen, which also served
as the background for Henry's painting. The music introduced
a galloping horse coming into the prairie landscape from afar,
while Harry was swiftly painting a horse with Chinese ink and
brush painting style. The audience was mesmerized by the complex multimedia performance switching from scene to scene for
twenty-five minutes.

When the largest painting was completed, Andy struck the
singing bowl, and the audience assumed the performance had
ended. However, before the pure metallic vibration of the singing
bowl had faded, Harry stepped behind the wet canvas. Taking out
a pocketknife, he started to cut a big opening in the centre of the
painting from behind while fresh ink was still dripping from the
wet canvas.

The audience was shocked. Some people made uncontrollable
noises, some covered up their mouths, while others stood up
from their seats, making helpless gestures about the unbelievable
ending, as if a comedy had suddenly ended with the tragic death
of the hero.

Harry was the first artist to go through the opening in the
canvas, followed by Linda, Bruce, and Andy. The team joined their
hands and bowed to the audience. By then, the audience were all
on their feet, giving the performers a standing ovation.

Three weeks after the performance, the team had their reunion.
By then, full summer colours had returned to the neighbourhood
of Markham Village. Linda parked her car on the side of the street
opposite Harry's home. Almost at the same time, Andy arrived

and parked behind her. "Hello, Linda!" Andy stepped out of his car before Linda did.

"Hey, Andy, you look radiant, you've got good news," Linda speculated.

"What? How did you know?" They walked toward Harry's house.

"It's written on your face and carried in your gait."

"You're kidding me, Poet," checking himself, Andy laughed, "Are you teasing me, Linda?"

"Well, well, we shall see." With a smile, Linda pushed open the door and they stepped into the hallway.

When Harry came out, Andy and Linda halted simultaneously. It had been only three weeks since they were together performing for the academic conference, but now Harry looked a totally different man standing before them. A black beard covered his face and joined his shoulder-length hair.

"Wow! Is that you, Harry?" Andy exclaimed.

"Are you doing a facelift?" Linda burst out laughing.

"Maybe, I just want to see how I look with a natural, long beard," Harry laughed with his friends. "Hey, what's the fuss, women change their hairstyles all the time."

"That's true," admitted Linda; she had added some red highlights to her own hair.

During their thirty minutes of meditation, Linda couldn't help but open her eyes several times to check on Harry's new look. She saw that his right arm was suspended in midair and the singing bowl lay on top of his right fist. Both men had cast their eyes down during meditation. Linda wondered if Harry was preparing himself for a new journey.

When they sat down at the table, sipping green tea and reflecting on their latest performance, Andy stood up abruptly from the table. "Excuse me for a few minutes, I don't want to forget about this." He walked toward the door leading to the basement.

"Turn on the lights, Andy," Harry called from the table.

In about five minutes, Andy came back up, empty handed but looking satisfied. "Harry, I must tell you, finally, I think I understood your student's artwork."

"What artwork?"

"*The Broken Mirror*, it is a piece of profound art."

Harry looked stunned.

"You did? OK, tell us about it. What did you rediscover today after coming to my house for two years?" Harry stood up from the table. "Let's all go down to the studio."

When they were standing in front of what actually resembled a complete jigsaw puzzle on the wall, Linda was as speechless as she was two years ago. Her memory was slowly refreshing itself as she focused on the numerous irregular pieces of broken mirror glued piece by piece inside the original frame.

"Tell us why you're suddenly interested in this artwork," Harry asked Andy. "What made you say it's a piece of profound art today?"

Clearing his throat, Andy gathered his thoughts, "OK, two years ago during the initial tour of the studio, I was quite puzzled by this piece. I couldn't understand why a reassembled broken mirror could be categorized as art. To me it didn't need much artistic skill." Andy paused, looking at Linda, inviting her to respond. She nodded to acknowledge the same feeling.

"But it was during our recent performance," Andy continued, "when you started to cut up the large painting on the stage, somehow I remembered the broken mirror and I had an insight about it."

Harry looked at Linda, they were both amazed by Andy's claim. "Go on," Harry urged.

"Harry, do you remember what you told the audience during the Q & A?"

Harry scratched his head, "Come on, you tell me."

Andy remarked thoughtfully, "You said your art is part of your spiritual journey. It should have nothing to do with an artist's ego."

"OK, but why is the broken mirror a piece of profound art. Wasn't the painting that I cut up on stage also profound?"

Andy looked at Linda, a smile was slowly appearing on her face. "I think I got it!"

"You did?" Harry asked. "What's the difference?"

"Mirror, mirror on the wall, who is the fairest of them all?" Linda replied.

"Thank you, Linda, for making such a handy reference to popular Disney culture." Harry turned to Andy, "Now you've made a symbolic assumption that a mirror provokes narcissistic self-interest in the artist."

"On the second level," Andy continued with his exploration, "if the artist broke the mirror intentionally, then he made a public statement, as we did on the stage, by cutting up the large painting."

"A good point," Linda said and picked up the discussion. "And thirdly, when the artist collected and glued the broken pieces of the mirror back into the frame, he created a different piece of new art. Somehow, he had given the demolished old mirror a new life, through the process of rebirth, isn't it?"

"Exactly! The rebirth motif again. Can you elaborate?" Harry was still leading the discussion to another level. Linda and Andy looked at each other, and Linda tried again to articulate. "After rebirth, the broken mirror no longer functions as a mirror, but is self-reflection. Therefore, its rebirth is meaningful in other ways than a simple repetition."

"Wow! You both are incredible art critics!" Harry exclaimed.

"Andy, thank you for sharing your spiritual enlightenment with us today," Linda said, "it has taken us two years to realize that an artist's spiritual hindrance is rooted in the ego."

"Well done! Fellow spiritual pursuers. *The Broken Mirror* is no doubt a piece of conceptual art. So was our performance. Now let's go upstairs. The tea is subtle and delicious and at its best right now," Harry urged.

Back at the table, sipping green tea slowly, a hearty smile slowly appeared on Andy's face. "Hey, fellow artists, I almost forgot to share my good news with you. I quit my job this morning!"

"You did? Congratulations!" Harry and Linda stood up to shake Andy's hand.

"Hey Andy, didn't I say earlier that you had good news?"

"You did, Linda, you said it exactly. I just couldn't believe it was true until now. But how did you know?"

Linda smiled. "When you stepped out of your car, it was written on your face and carried in your gait. I sensed it, because you have wanted to move on to something more meaningful."

"What will you be doing, Andy? From now on, you are your own boss," Harry said.

"I want to work full-time on Moon Pointing Productions."

"Great, what exactly are you planning to do?"

"I plan to launch an official website, start a meditation program, invite people of different religions and faiths to attend, invite speakers, maybe organize interfaith events, and so on."

"Sounds interesting and ambitious, what about funding?"

"Meditation sessions will be free of charge to attend, since they will be held in local parks and the community centre. For events with speakers, we may ask people for donations."

"Good luck, Andy," Linda said cheerfully. "Don't forget it takes years to build a business. Maybe one day you will open a specialty store to sell meditation cushions."

"That's right, that was my initial idea for a business. I won't forget that."

"Following Andy," Harry cuts in with a smile, "I might as well make an announcement. This summer I will travel to Japan and

Taiwan to practice meditation, then to Hong Kong and China to visit some artist friends. In early fall, I need to go to New York City for an art event. And starting this fall, I will concentrate on preparing for my solo exhibitions in Hong Kong this winter and in Vancouver next spring. I won't be able to participate in our regular meetings or performances for some time."

Linda was holding her head within her cupped hands, her elbows on the table. Intuitively, she had sensed that the time for them to move away from each other had finally come. The necessity of timely departure from the group would further each person's spiritual pursuit, artistic practice, and business endeavour, making future developments more contingent on personal responsibility and experience.

"What about you, Linda?" Andy asked softly, sounding concerned. "Do you have any plans?"

"Mm, I will write a story about a group of spiritual pursuers, who crossed each other's paths meaningfully for a couple of years in their lives," Linda answered with a smile.

Author's Note

When I started this new collection in 2015, I envisioned globalization as the overall background for the stories. The ripple effects of China's economic success in the past four decades have left incremental impacts on Canadians. My essential interest remains to witness and record the nouveau, social, economic, and technological changes worldwide in our lifetime that have made impacts on who we are and what we value.

During the years 2020-2022 the Coronavirus pandemic threatened the very survival of humanity. The world underwent a tremendous turmoil, with much suffering and loss of lives, collective confidence, fundamental optimism, and individual freedom. Globalization has lost its vitality; and its legitimacy has been seriously questioned and further undermined by the Russian invasion of Ukraine in February 2022.

During the seemingly endless days of quarantine, I have worked and reworked on my stories, rewriting and expanding the original short stories into long stories or novellas. I have also revised a forgotten manuscript initially drafted in 2008. Hence, I have five novellas for this new collection.

Cultural interactions among Canadians of different racial, cultural, and spiritual backgrounds are the essential interest and focus of my stories. The characters are inspired by real life models and depicted from various walks of life in the greater metropolitan Toronto area and its satellite cities. "An Abiding Dream" describes older Chinese Canadians who lived and worked in the downtown Chinatown area. The artists among them cherished "An Abiding Dream" to share their art with the broader Canadian society. In the late 1980s, some portrait artists organized a mixed racial group of immigrants to work at the Yonge/Dundas street corner of downtown Toronto. This story was initially drafted after my interviews with two members of the group in 2008. In the latest revision, I have updated the timeline to the spring of 2020, when I recalled the last concern of the interviewees, "Don't let our history be forgotten."

"Under the Big Tree" and "Five W and H" both depicted the ripple effects of China's economic reform and success on Canadian men and women, white and blue-collar, employed and retired, as well as freelance artists. The reader will learn the Chinese slang term, *da wan*, referring to the extremely wealthy Mainland Chinese businessmen and businesswomen. When a group of local Canadian artists met with a *da wan* artist from China, they naïvely believed they would be able to share the former's business network and personal list of collectors in China's fast-growing art markets.

I chose "Five W and H"—a well-known journalistic formula—as the title for the third story, so that the readers can follow a large group of ordinary Canadians, who blindly bought a "diamond" membership from an old Canadian company that promised to bring lucrative retail business opportunities in China to its members. The novella starts with "Where we live" and ends with "Who we are." The scheme failed, and the Canadian company closed down permanently, without an official statement. What had happened? And why? The members and the readers were left to figure out their own answers.

The title of "Leftover Women" was borrowed from an official Chinese term in circulation in the past decade when referring to single, never-married women between ages 27 and 44. This derogatory term was renounced by most Canadian women upon hearing it; however, it did echo as a personal experience by many single women. Underlining the dilemma were not only personal and familial conflicts, but also gender bias and discrimination in our social milieu regarding women's age, marital status, and personal choices.

After working and reworking with the stories, I realized I actually knew all the characters, among them, I knew some characters intimately well, because they are also artists. I valued the opportunities to work with fellow artists of different disciplines in joint projects. The title story "Spiritual Pursuits" follows the paths of three artists over three years. Their personal growth and joint artistic projects were intertwined in the weekly group meditations, discussions, and artistic creation, which they shared with the public at communal events.

I would like to express my heartfelt gratitude to my dear artist friend, Mr Wang De Hui, who has granted permission to use his famous oil painting, *Sunset on the Desert* 大漠落日* (2005) as the cover art for this new book. Most of De Hui's lifetime art collections of oil paintings and Chinese brush paintings have long been permanently collected in the Zhejiang Art Museum in China.

I would also like to thank my publisher Mawenzi House for their encouragement along my writing career. I thank them for

---

* *Sunset on the Desert* 大漠落日 by Wang De Hui, 73cmx90cm, oil on canvas, 2005. Reproduced from *Wang De Hui* 王德惠. Ed. Wang Kun & Wang Shaoqiu. Hangzhou: China Academy of Fine Arts Publishing House, 2014. Pp. 204-205.

honouring Wang De Hui's oil painting, which best embodies the journey motif in all my five stories. I was delighted that my daughter Avianna Chao offered to handle the difficult digital scanning of the image from the huge hardcover collection entitled *Wang De Hui*, published by China Academy of Fine Arts in 2014. I also thank my friend Brian Fanslow in Texas, who was the first reader of the manuscript, and fellow artist Henry Ho, who gifted me 問道緣 as the potential title for the future Chinese version of the book. I am grateful to the Ontario Arts Council for supporting this project with the Recommender Grants for Writers.

Finally, I wish to honour the community of Asian Heritage Month artists including painters, writers, poets, musicians, photographers, performers, and digital artists for their inspiring art projects created and shared virtually with the public during the three years of COVID-19 pandemic shut down. Here is an incomplete list of names: Arlene Chan, Ka Nin Chan, Leo Chan, Philip Chan, Avianna Chao, Tam Kam Chiu, Sharon Cook, Patrick Haynes, Alice Ho, Edwin Ho, Henry Ho, Irene Hung, Leona Lai, Linda Lai, Kay Li, Peter Lo, Weiping Lu, Ashley Poy, Joe Rivera, Patria Rivera, Madeleine Thien, and Paul Yee.

Vincent van Gogh once said, "I am searching, I am striving, I am putting myself in it." I believe we did exactly that, jointly.

Lien Chao
Toronto, Canada
Spring 2023

Also by Lien Chao

Salt in My Life, bilingual poetry (2019)

The Chinese Knot and Other Stories (2008)

More Than Skin Deep, bilingual poetry (2004)

Strike the Work: An Anthology of Contemporary Chinese Canadian Fiction (with Jim Wong-Chu, 2003)

Tiger Girl (Hu Nü), creative memoir (2001)

Maples and the Stream, bilingual poetry (1999)

Beyond Silence: Chinese Canadian Literature in English (1997)